## "About Last Night," Charles Said. "I've Had A Change Of Heart."

*Uh oh.*

"Now that I know what I'll be missing," he added, "maybe I won't be cooperating with the royal family after all."

Oh yes, kissing him had been a really bad idea.

He was coming closer with that look in his eyes, like any second he planned to ravish her. And she wanted him to. Desperately.

He'd managed to turn the tables on her.

"I mean, what's the worst that can happen?" he said.

Hopefully something really bad. "Renouncement? Hanging?" she offered.

He only smiled. He was standing so close now that he could reach out and touch her.

Dear Reader,

Welcome to book four of my ROYAL SEDUCTIONS series! The story of Charles Mead, Duke of Morgan Isle, and his personal assistant, Victoria Houghton.

I've never been the corporate type—most days I don't change out of my pajamas until it's time to make dinner—so Victoria intrigued me from the start. She's so confident and determined. And tough. At least, that was what I saw, until I scratched the surface and realized that she has just as many insecurities as the rest of us. And Charles, a shameless and hopeless flirt, uses every single one to his advantage.

Their interactions are intense, their dialogue witty and sharp, and their physical attraction off the charts. It was fun to sit back and see who would tackle whom first. It might surprise you.

You'll even meet a new family member…but I don't want to give too much away. I hope you enjoy it!

I'll see you again in July for the next book in the ROYAL SEDUCTIONS series, when you'll meet the royal family of Thomas Isle, and their crown prince, the *Royal Seducer,* who also happens to be Desire's MAN OF THE MONTH!

Best,

*Michelle*

# THE DUKE'S
# BOARDROOM
# AFFAIR

## MICHELLE CELMER

Published by Silhouette Books
**America's Publisher of Contemporary Romance**

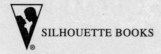

SILHOUETTE BOOKS

ISBN-13: 978-0-373-76919-3
ISBN-10:    0-373-76919-9

Recycling programs
for this product may
not exist in your area.

THE DUKE'S BOARDROOM AFFAIR

Visit Silhouette Books at www.eHarlequin.com

**Printed in U.S.A.**

**Books by Michelle Celmer**

Silhouette Desire

*The Millionaire's Pregnant Mistress* #1739
*The Secretary's Secret* #1774
*Best Man's Conquest* #1799
*\*The King's Convenient Bride* #1876
*\*The Illegitimate Prince's Baby* #1877
*\*An Affair with the Princess* #1900
*\*The Duke's Boardroom Affair* #1919

Silhouette Romantic Suspense

*Running On Empty* #1342
*Out of Sight* #1398

Silhouette Special Edition

*Accidentally Expecting* #1847

*Royal Seductions

## MICHELLE CELMER

Bestselling author Michelle Celmer lives in southeastern Michigan with her husband, their three children, two dogs and two cats. When she's not writing or busy being a mom, you can find her in the garden or curled up with a romance novel. And if you twist her arm real hard you can usually persuade her into a day of power shopping.

Michelle loves to hear from readers. Visit her Web site at www.michellecelmer.com, or write her at P.O. Box 300, Clawson, MI 48017.

To my Aunt Janet, who,
besides being totally cool and tons of fun,
told me my first dirty joke when I was a kid.
Why does a honeymoon only last six days?
I think you remember the rest....

# One

Victoria Houghton had never been so humiliated.

Watching her father lose in a hostile takeover the hotel that had been in their family for generations had been almost more than she could bear—and now she was expected to be a personal assistant to the man who was instrumental in sealing the deal?

The Duke of Morgan Isle, Charles Frederick Mead, lounged casually behind his desk, smug and arrogant beneath the facade of a charming smile, the crisp blue of the Irish Sea a backdrop a wall of floor-to-ceiling office windows behind him. Dressed in a suit that was no doubt custom-made, his casual stance was at odds with the undeniable air of authority he oozed from every pore.

"I was told I would be taking on a managerial

position," she told him. And along with it a generous salary and profit sharing. Or had they changed their minds about that part, too?

He leaned back and folded one leg casually atop the other. "Until the second phase of the hotel opens, there's nothing for you to manage. And since my personal assistant recently left, you will temporarily replace her."

He must have thought her daft if he believed she would buy that flimsy excuse. She would work in housekeeping, changing linens and scrubbing commodes, if it meant not seeing this man every day. He may have looked pleasant and easygoing, but underneath he was cold and heartless.

"So put me in the part of the hotel that's already completed," she said. "I'll do anything."

"There aren't any openings."

*"None?"*

He shook his head.

Of course there weren't. Or so he said. To men like him, lying was as natural as breathing. And what of their financial agreement? Surely he didn't expect to pay an assistant the exorbitant salary they had quoted in her contract? "What about my salary and profit sharing?"

He shrugged. "Nothing in the terms of your contract will change."

Her brow perked up in surprise. What was he trying to pull?

"If you consult your attorney, he'll confirm that we're honoring our end of the deal," he assured her.

According to her father, their own attorney had sold them out to get in good with the royal family, so unfortunately he wouldn't be much help. She doubted there was a single attorney on the island who would take on the monarchy, so basically, she was screwed.

"And if I refuse?" she asked, though she already knew the answer.

"You violate the terms of your contract."

He had no idea how tempted she was to do just that. She'd never wanted this job. But refusing it would devastate her father. The sale of his hotel—her legacy—to the royal family for their expansion project had been contingent on her being hired as a permanent manager, and at nearly twice the salary she had been making before. Not to mention incredible benefits. He wanted assurances that she would be well taken care of. And she was helpless to object.

Losing the hotel had put unneeded strain on his already weakening heart. Despite sitting on the prime resort land of the island, since the opening of the newly renovated Royal Inn hotel, occupancy in their much smaller facility had begun to drop. The way the lawyers for the royal family had begun buying up ocean-side property, both she and her father feared it would only be a matter of time before their number was up.

And they had been right.

In his fragile state, more bad news might be all it took to do him in. Since the day her mother and older brother were killed in an automobile accident, when Victoria was only five, he had been her entire life. He had sacrificed so much for her. She couldn't let him down.

With renewed resolve, she squared her shoulders and asked, "When do you expect the second phase of the hotel to open?"

"The additions and renovations are scheduled for completion by the beginning of the next tourist season."

The next tourist season? But that was nearly six months away! Six *days* would be too long to work for this man, as far as she was concerned. But what choice did she have?

Something that looked like amusement sparked in his deep, chocolate-brown eyes. Did he think this was funny?

"Is that a problem?" he asked.

She realized the duke was baiting her. He *wanted* her to violate the terms of her contract so he could get rid of her. He didn't want her services any more than she wanted his charity.

Well, she wouldn't give him the satisfaction of seeing her buckle. He may have broken her father, but there was no way he was going to break her.

She raised her chin a notch and looked him directly in the eye, so he would see that she wasn't intimidated. "No problem."

"Excellent." A satisfied and, though she hated to admit it, *sexy* grin curled the corners of his mouth. Which she didn't doubt was exactly what he wanted her to think.

He opened the top drawer of his desk, extracted a form of some sort, and slid it toward her. "You'll need to sign this."

She narrowed her eyes at him. "What is it?"

"Our standard nondisclosure agreement. Every employee of the royal family is obligated to sign one."

Another trick? But after a quick scan of the document, she realized it was a very simple, basic agreement. And though she wouldn't be working directly for the royal family but instead for the hotel chain they now owned, she didn't feel it was worth arguing. Their secrets would be safe with her.

Yet, as she took the gold-plated pen he offered and signed her name, she couldn't escape the feeling that she had just sold her soul to the devil.

She handed it back to him and he tucked it inside his desk, then he rose from his chair. Short as she was, she was used to looking up to meet people in the eye, but he towered over her. At least a foot and a half taller than her measly five foot one. And he looked so…perfect. His suit an exact fit, his nails neatly trimmed and buffed, not a strand of his closely cropped, jet-black hair out of place.

But men like him were never as perfect as they appeared. God knows she'd met her share of imperfect men. Despite his looks and money and power, he was just as flawed as the next guy. Probably more so. And being that he was an attorney, she wouldn't trust him as far as she could throw him—which, considering their size difference, wouldn't be very far.

"Welcome to the company, Victoria." He extended a hand for her to shake and, determined to be professional, she accepted it.

His hand enfolded her own, gobbling it up, big and warm and firm. And she felt a strange stirring in the pit of her belly. A kind of fluttering tickle.

His hand still gripping hers, he said, "Why don't we discuss your duties over lunch?" But his eyes said he had more than just lunch in mind. Was he *hitting* on her?

*You have got to be kidding me*.

She came this close to rolling her eyes. The tabloids

were forever painting him as a shameless, ruthless womanizer, but she had always assumed that was just gossip. No man could possibly be that shallow. Perhaps, though, they weren't so far off the mark.

If he believed for an instant that he would be adding her to his list of female conquests, he was delusional.

As graciously as possible she pried her hand loose. "No. Thank you."

He regarded her curiously. Maybe he wasn't used to women telling him no. "My treat," he said, dangling the word in front of her like bait.

Did he really think she was that hard up?

"We're going to be working somewhat closely," he added, and she could swear she heard a hint of emphasis on *closely*. "We should take the time to get to know one another."

They wouldn't be working *that* closely. "I prefer not to mix business with pleasure."

She wondered if he would insist, citing it as part of their contract, but he only shrugged and stepped around his desk. "Well, then, I'll show you to your office."

Instead of taking her back through the outer office, past the grim-faced, aged secretary she'd met on the way in, he led her through a different door to a smaller, sparsely decorated, windowless office with little more than an empty bookcase, a comfortable-looking leather office chair, and an adequately sized desk. On it's surface sat a phone, a laptop computer and a large manila envelope.

"Everything you need is on your computer," he explained. "You'll find a list of all your duties, along with any phone numbers you may need as well as a copy of my personal schedule. If you're unsure of how to use the program you can ask Penelope, my secretary, for help."

"I'm sure I can figure it out."

He picked up the envelope and handed it to her. "Inside is a badge for this building, and another that will give you access to the business offices at the palace—"

"The *palace?*" She never imagined that going to the palace would be a part of the job description.

"I keep an office there and often attend meetings with King Phillip. Have you ever been there?"

She shook her head. She'd only seen photographs. Not that she hadn't imagined what it would be like.

"Well, then, I'll have to give you a tour."

Okay, maybe there would be *some* perks to this job. The idea of being in the palace, and possibly meeting members of the royal family, filled her with nervous excitement. Then she reined in her wayward emotions by reminding herself that this was not going to be a fun job. And given the choice, she would rather be anywhere but here.

"You'll also find a set of card keys," he continued, "for both your office and mine. They're marked accordingly. And in a separate envelope is your personal security code for my house."

Why on earth would he give her access to his house?

"My driver will be at your disposal twenty-four hours a day. Unless, of course, I'm using him, in which case you will be reimbursed for your petrol use."

A driver? She couldn't imagine what she would need that for. This job just kept getting stranger and stranger.

He gestured to a second door, adjacent to the one connecting their offices.

"That door leads to Penelope's office and will be the entrance that you use. She'll take you on a tour of the building, show you the break room and facilities. If you need to speak to me specifically, call first. The line to my office is marked on the phone. If I don't answer that means I'm busy and not to be disturbed."

"All right."

"My business calls go through Penelope, but any personal calls will be routed through your office or to the cell phone I'll supply you."

Answering phones and taking messages? Not the most challenging job in the world. But the duke was obviously a man who liked things done a certain way, and if nothing else she respected that. More than once her employees at the Houghton had suggested she was a little too rigid when it came to her business practices, but she had never felt an ounce of regret for running a tight ship.

She had been working since the age of twelve, when her father let her help out in the Houghton Hotel office after school. But only after earning her master's degree in business at university was she promoted to manager. Her father had insisted she earn her education, should she ever need something to fall back on.

And, boy, had she fallen back.

"Take some time to look over your duties, then we can discuss any questions you have," he said.

"Fine."

"I have to warn you, I've been without an assistant for a week now, and I'm afraid things are in a bit of a mess."

Honestly, how hard could it be, being a glorified secretary? "I'm sure I can manage."

"Well," the Duke said, with one of those dazzling smiles, "I'll leave you to it, then."

He turned and was halfway through the door before she realized she had no idea how she was supposed to address him. Did she call him Sir, or Sire? Did she have to bow or curtsy?

"Excuse me," she said.

He turned back to her. "Yes?"

"What should I call you?" He looked puzzled, so she added, "Mr. or Sir? Your Highness?"

That grin was back, and, like his handshake, she felt it all the way to the pit of her belly.

*Stop that,* she warned herself. He only smiled that way because he *wanted* her to feel it in her belly.

"Let's go with Charles," he said.

She wasn't sure if that was proper. Calling him by his first name just felt too…casual. But he was calling the shots, and she wasn't going to give him any reason to accuse her of violating the contract. "All right."

He flashed her one last smile before he closed the door behind him, and she had the distinct feeling he knew something she didn't. Or maybe that was just part of the game. Either way, she refused to let him intimidate her. If they thought they were going to force her out, they had no idea who they were dealing with. She hadn't earned her reputation as a savvy businesswoman by letting people walk all over her.

She took a seat at her new desk, finding the chair to be as comfortable as it looked. But the office itself was cold and impersonal. Since she would be spending at least six months here, it wouldn't hurt to bring a few photos and personal items into work.

She opened the laptop and booted it up. On the desktop were the documents he had mentioned. Convinced this job couldn't get any worse, she opened the one titled *Duties*. Starting at the top, she read her job description, working her way down the two-page, single-spaced list, her stomach sinking lower with each line, until she could swear it slipped all the way down near the balls of her feet. *Personal assistant, my foot.*

She had just agreed to be Charles Frederick Mead's indentured slave.

# Two

Charles sat at his desk, watching the time tick by on his Rolex. He gave Victoria five minutes before she stormed into his office in a snit about her employment duties. And he'd bet his ample net worth that she'd forget to call first.

For a woman with her education and experience, the backward step from managing a five-hundred-room hotel to the duties of a personal assistant would be tough to navigate. If it were up to him, he'd have found her a position in the hotel. But it wasn't his call. His cousins, King Phillip and Prince Ethan, were calling the shots.

The Houghton Hotel hadn't been acquired under the best of circumstances—at least, not for the Houghton family—and the royal family needed to know if Victoria was trustworthy before they allowed her into the fold. The logical way to do that was to keep her close.

He could see that she was still distraught over the loss of their hotel and property, but, sadly, the buyout had been inevitable. If not the Royal Inn, some other establishment would have swooped in for the kill. At least with the royal family they were given a fair deal. Other prospective buyers, with less interest in the country's economy, might have been far less accommodating. But it was possible that Victoria and her father, Reginald Houghton, didn't see it that way. But at the very least, she could show a little bit of gratitude. The royal family had saved them the embarrassment of both professional and personal financial devastation.

He'd barely completed the thought when his phone rang. Three short chirps, indicating the call originated from Victoria's office. She remembered.

He glanced at his watch. She was early. Only three and a half minutes.

He answered with a patient, "Yes, Victoria."

"I'm ready to discuss my duties," she said, and there was a distinct undertone of tension in her voice that made him grin.

"That was quick," he said. "Come on in."

The door opened a second later, and she emerged, a look on her face that could only be described as *determined*. For a woman her size, barely more than a nymph, she had a presence that overwhelmed a room. A firestorm of attitude and spunk packed neatly into a petite and, dare he say, *sexy* package. He usually preferred women with long, silky hair—and typically blond—but her shorter, warm brown, sassy style seemed to fit her just right.

He wasn't typically drawn to strong-willed women, but Victoria fascinated him. And he wouldn't mind at all getting to know her better. Which he would, despite what she seemed to believe. It was a simple fact: women found him irresistible. It was exhausting at times, really, the way women threw themselves at him. He didn't help matters by encouraging them. But he just couldn't help himself. He loved everything about women: Their soft curves and the silky warmth of their skin. The way they smelled and tasted. In fact, when it came to the female form, there wasn't a single thing he didn't adore.

This time, he had his sights set on Victoria. And he had yet to meet a woman he couldn't seduce.

"You have questions?" he asked her.

"A few."

He leaned back in his chair and folded his arms. "Let's hear it."

She seemed to choose her words very carefully. "I assumed my duties would be limited to more of a…secretarial nature."

"I have a secretary. What you'll be doing is handling every aspect of my private affairs. From fetching my dry cleaning to screening my e-mail and calls. Making dinner reservations and booking events. If I need a gift for a friend or flowers for a date, it will be your responsibility to make it happen. You'll also accompany me to any business meetings where I might require you to take notes."

She nodded slowly, and he could see that she was struggling to keep her cool. "I understand that you need to fill the position, but don't you think I'm a little *over*-qualified?"

He flashed her a patient and sympathetic smile. "I realize this is quite a step down from what you're used to. But as I said before, until the second phase opens…" He shrugged, lifting his hands in a gesture of helplessness. "If it's any consolation, since my last assistant left, my life has been in shambles. There will be plenty to keep you busy."

For a second she looked as though she might press the issue, then thought better of it. It wasn't often anyone outside of the family contradicted him. It was just a part of the title.

She spared him a stiff, strained smile. "Well, then, I guess I should get started."

He was sure that once she got going, she would find managing his life something of a challenge. He wished he could say the same for seducing her, but he had the sneaking suspicion it would be all too easy.


Charles hadn't been kidding when he said his life was in shambles.

After a quick tour of the building with Penelope, who had the personality and warmth of an iceberg, Victoria started at the top of his to do list. Sorting his e-mail. She had to go through his personal account and first weed out the spam that had slipped through the filter, then compare the sender addresses on legitimate mail to a list of people whose e-mails were to be sorted into several separate categories. Which didn't sound like much of an undertaking, until she opened the account and discovered over *four hundred* e-mails awaiting her attention.

There were dozens from charities requesting his donation or endorsement, and notes from family and friends, including at least three or four a day from his mother. A lot of e-mails from women. And others from random people who admired him or in some cases didn't speak too fondly of him. Cross-referencing them all with the list of addresses he'd supplied her would be a tedious, time-consuming task. And it seemed as though for every e-mail she erased or filed, a new one would appear in his inbox.

When eyestrain and fatigue had her vision blurring, she took a break and moved down to number two on the list. His voice mail. Following his instructions, she dialed the number and punched in the PIN, and was nearly knocked out of her chair when the voice announced that he had two hundred and twenty-six new messages! She didn't get that many personal calls in a month, much less a week. And she couldn't help wondering how many of those calls were from women.

It didn't take long to find out.

There was Amber from the hotel bar, Jennifer from the club, Alexis from the ski lodge, and half a dozen more. Most rang more than once, sounding a bit more desperate and needy with each message. The lead offender for repeated calls, however, was Charles's mother. She seemed to follow up every e-mail she sent with a phone call, or maybe it was the other way around. No less than *three* times a day. Sometimes more. And she began every call the exact same way. *It's your mum. I know you're busy, but I wanted to tell you...*

Nothing pressing as far as Victoria could tell. Just

random tidbits about family or friends, or reminders of events he had promised to attend. A very attractive woman from a good family she would like him to meet. And she seemed to have an endless variety of pet names for him. Pumpkin and Sweetie. Love and Precious. Although Victoria's favorite by far was Lamb Chop.

His mother never requested, or seemed to expect, a return call, and her messages dripped with a syrupy sweetness that made Victoria's skin crawl. How could Charles stand it?

Easily. By having someone else check his messages.

She spent the next couple of hours listening to the first hundred or so calls, transcribing the messages for Charles, including a return phone number should he need to answer the call. Any incoming calls she let go directly to voice until she had time to catch up. Between the e-mail and voice mail, it could take days.

"Working late?"

Startled by the unexpected intrusion, she nearly dropped the phone. She looked up to find Charles standing in the doorway between their two offices. She couldn't help but wonder how long he'd been standing there watching her.

"I'm sorry, what?" she said, setting the phone back in the cradle.

Her reaction seemed to amuse him. "I asked if you're working late."

She looked at her watch and realized that it was nearly eight p.m. She'd worked clear through lunch and dinner. "I guess I lost track of the hour."

"You're not required to work overtime."

"I have a lot of work to catch up on." Besides, she would much rather have been busy working than sitting home alone in the flat she had been forced to rent when her father could no longer afford to keep the family estate. Since she was born, that house had been the only place she had ever called home. But there was a new family living there now. Strangers occupying the rooms that were meant to belong to her own children some day.

Every time she set foot in her new residence, it was a grim, stark reminder of everything they had lost. And Charles, she reminded herself, was the catalyst.

He held up what she assumed was to be her new phone. The most expensive, state-of-the-art gadget on the market. "Before Penelope left she brought this in."

She felt a sudden wave of alarm. His secretary was gone? Meaning they were alone?

She wondered who else was in the building, and if working alone with him was wise. She barely knew him.

"Is everyone gone?" she asked in a voice that she hoped sounded nonchalant.

"This is a law firm. There's always someone working late on a case or an intern pulling an overnighter. If it's safety you're concerned about, the parking structure is monitored by cameras around the clock, and we employ a security detail in the lobby twenty-four seven."

"Oh, that's good to know." Still, as he walked toward her desk to hand her the mobile phone, she tensed the tiniest bit. He was just so tall and assuming. So...*there*.

"It's a PDA as well as a phone. And you can check e-mail and browse the Internet. If you take it to Nigel in tech support on the fourth floor tomorrow morning, he'll set everything up for you."

"Okay." As she took it from him their fingers touched and she had to force herself not to jerk away. It was barely a brush; still, she felt warmth and electricity shoot across the surface of her skin. Which made no sense considering how much she disliked him.

"I've been going through your phone messages," she told him. "Your mother called. Many times."

"Well, there's a surprise," he said, a definite note of exasperation in his voice. "I should probably warn you that when it comes to dealing with my mother, you have to be firm or she'll walk all over you."

"I can do that." Being *firm* had never been a problem for her. In fact, there had been instances when she'd been accused of being *too* firm. A necessity for any woman in a position of power. She had learned very early in her career how not to let people walk all over her.

"Good." He glanced at his watch. "I'm on my way out, and since it would seem that neither of us has eaten yet, why don't you let me take you out to dinner?"

First a lunch invitation, now dinner? Couldn't he take no for an answer? "No, thank you."

Her rejection seemed to amuse him. He shrugged and said, "Have it your way."

What was that supposed to mean? Whose *way* did he expect her to have it? His?

"I'm going to the dry cleaners tomorrow to pick up your laundry," she said. "Do you have anything dirty at home that I should take with me?"

"I do, actually. My housekeeper is off tomorrow

morning but I'll try to remember to set it by the door before I leave for work. Would you like my car to pick you up?"

"I can drive myself." Her father had always had a driver—until recently, anyway—but she never had felt comfortable having someone chauffer her around. She was too independent. She liked to be in control of her environment and her destiny. Which had been much easier when her father owned the company. When she was in charge. Answering to the whims of someone else was going to be...a *challenge*.

He shrugged again. "If that's what you prefer. I guess I'll see you in the morning."

Unfortunately, yes, he would. And nearly every morning for the following six months. "Good night."

For several very long seconds he just looked at her, then he flashed her one of those devastating, sexy smiles before he walked out of her office, shutting the door behind him.

And despite her less-than-sparkling opinion of him, she couldn't help feeling just a tiny bit breathless.

Victoria checked her caller ID when she got home and saw that her father had called several times. No doubt wondering how her first day had gone. All she wanted to do was fall into bed and sleep, but if she didn't call him back he would worry. She dialed his number, knowing she would have to tread lightly, choose her words carefully, so as not to upset him.

He answered sounding wounded and upset. "I thought you wouldn't call."

It struck her how old he sounded. Too frail for a man of sixty-five. He used to be so strong and gregarious. Lately he seemed to be fading away. "Why wouldn't I call?"

"I thought you might be cross with me for making you take that job. I know it couldn't have been easy, working for those people."

That was the way he'd referred to the royal family lately. *Those people.* "I've told you a million times, Daddy, that I am not upset. It's a good job. Where else would I make such a generous salary? If it does well, the profit sharing will make me a very wealthy woman." She found it only slightly ironic that she was regurgitating the same words he had used to convince her to take the position in the first place.

"I know," he conceded. "But no salary, no matter how great, could make up for what was stolen from us."

And she knew that he would live with that regret for the rest of his life. All she could do was continually assure him that it wasn't his fault. Yet, regardless of whose mistake it was, she couldn't help feeling that she would spend the rest of her life paying for it.

"Is it a nice hotel?" he asked grudgingly.

"Well, I didn't actually see the hotel yet."

"Why not?"

Oh, boy, this was going to be tough to explain. "There isn't a manager's position open in the hotel right now," she said, and told him about the job with the duke, stressing that her contract wouldn't change.

"That is completely unacceptable," he said, and she could practically feel his blood pressure rising, could just imagine the veins at his temples pulsing. He'd already had two heart attacks. One more could be fatal.

"It's fine, Daddy. Honestly."

"Would you like me to contact my attorney?"

For all the good that would do her. "No."

"Are you sure? There must be something he can do."

Was he forgetting that it was his attorney who was partially to blame for getting them into this mess?

"There's no need, Daddy. It's not so bad, really. In fact, I think it might be something of a challenge. A nice change of pace."

He accepted her lie, and some of the tension seemed to slip from his voice. He changed the subject and they went on to talk about an upcoming party for a family friend, and she tried to remain upbeat and cheerful. By the time she hung up she felt exhausted from the effort.

Performing her duties would be taxing enough, but she could see that creating a ruse to keep her father placated would be a long and arduous task. But what choice did she have? She was all her father had left in the world. He had sacrificed so much for her. Made her the center of his universe.

No matter what, she *couldn't* let him down.

# Three

Charles lived in an exclusive, heavily gated and guarded community fifteen miles up the coast in the city of Pine Bluff. His house, a towering structure of glass and stone, sat in the arc of a cul-de-sac on the bluff overlooking the ocean. It was a lot of house for a single man, but that hardly surprised her. She was sure he had money to burn.

Victoria pulled her car up the circular drive and parked by the front door. She climbed out and took in the picturesque scenery, filled her lungs with clean, salty autumn air. If nothing else, the duke had impeccable taste in real estate. As well as interior design, she admitted to herself, after she used her code to open the door and stepped inside the foyer. Warm beiges and deep hues of green and blue welcomed her inside. The foyer opened up into a spacious living room with a rustic stone fireplace that climbed to the peak of a steep cathedral ceiling. It should have looked out of place with the modern design, but instead it gave the room warmth and character.

She had planned to grab the laundry and be on her way, but the bag he had said he would leave by the door was conspicuously not there. Either he hadn't left yet or he'd forgotten. She was guessing the latter.

"Hello!" she called, straining to hear for any signs of life, but the house was silent. She would have to find the clothes herself, and the logical place to look would be his bedroom.

She followed the plushly carpeted staircase up to the second floor and down an open hallway that overlooked the family room below. The home she had grown up in was more traditional in design, but she liked the open floor plan of Charles's house.

"Hello!" she called again, and got no answer. With the option of going either left or right, she chose right and peered into each of the half-dozen open doors. Spare rooms, mostly. But at the end of the hall she hit the jackpot. The master suite.

It was decorated just as warmly as the living room, but definitely more masculine. An enormous sleigh bed—unmade, she noted—carved from deep, rich cherry dominated the center of the room. And the air teemed with the undeniable scent of the woodsy cologne he had been wearing the day before.

She tried one more firm "Hello! Anyone here?" and was met with silence.

Looked like the coast was clear.

Feeling like an interloper, she stepped inside, wondering where the closet might be hiding. She found it off the bathroom, an enormous space in which row upon row of suits in the finest and most beautiful fabrics she had ever seen hung neatly in order by color. Beside them hung his work shirts, and beside them stood a rack that must have had three hundred different ties hanging from its bars. She wondered if he had worn them all. The opposite side of the closet seemed casual in nature, and in the back she discovered a mountain of dirty clothes overflowing from a hamper conveniently marked Dry Cleaning.

It was shirts mostly. White, beige, and a few pale blue. She also noted that his scent was much stronger here. And strangely familiar. Not the scent of a man she had known only a day. Perhaps she knew someone who wore the same brand.

Purely out of curiosity she picked up one of the shirts and held it to her face, inhaling deeply.

"I see you found my laundry."

She was so startled by the unexpected voice that she squealed with surprise and spun around, but the heel of her pump caught in the carpet and she toppled over into a row of neatly hung trousers, taking several pairs with her as she landed with a thump on the floor.

Cheeks flaming with embarrassment, she looked up to find Charles standing over her, wearing nothing but a damp towel around his slim hips and an amused smile.

She quickly averted her gaze, but not before she registered a set of ridiculously defined abs, perfectly formed pecs, wide, sturdy shoulders, and biceps to die for. Damn her pesky photographic memory.

"I didn't mean to startle you," he said. He reached out a hand to help her up and she was so tangled she had no choice but to accept it.

"What are you doing here?" she snapped when she was back on her feet.

He shrugged. "I live here."

She averted her eyes, pretending to smooth the creases from her skirt, so she wouldn't have to look at all that sculpted perfection. "I'd assumed you'd left for work."

"It's only seven-forty-five."

"I called out but no one answered."

"The granite in the master bath was sealed yesterday, so I was using the spare room down the hall."

"Sorry," she mumbled, running out of places to look, without him realizing she was deliberately not looking at him.

"Something wrong with that shirt?" he asked.

She was still clutching the shirt she had picked up from the hamper, and she realized he must have seen her sniffing it. What could possibly be more embarrassing?

"I was checking to see if it was dirty," she said, cringing inwardly at that ridiculously flimsy excuse.

Charles grinned. "Well then, for future reference, I don't make a habit of keeping clean clothes in the hamper."

"I'll remember that." And she would make a mental note to never come into his house until she was entirely sure he wasn't there, or at the very least fully clothed. "Well, I'll get out of your way."

She turned and grabbed the rest of the clothes from the hamper, stacking them in her arms. He stepped out of her way and she rushed past him and through the doorway.

"Might as well stick around," he said.

She stopped and turned to him, saw that he was leaning casually in the closet doorway. She struggled to keep her eyes from wandering below his neck. "Why?"

"I was going to call my driver, but since you're here, I'll just catch a ride into work with you."

He wanted to ride with *her?* "I would, but, um, I have to stop at the dry cleaners first. I don't want to get you to work late."

"I don't mind." He ran his fingers through the damp, shiny waves of his hair, his biceps flexing under sun-bronzed skin. She stood there transfixed by the fluidity of his movements. His pecs looked hard and defined, and were sprinkled with fine, dark hair.

He may have been an arrogant ass, but God, he was a beautiful one.

"Give me five minutes," he said, and she nodded numbly, hoping her mouth wasn't hanging open, drool dripping from the corner.

"There's coffee in the kitchen," he added, then he turned back into the closet, already loosening the knot at his waist.

The last thing she saw, as he disappeared inside, was the towel drop to the floor, and the tantalizing curve of one perfectly formed butt cheek.

Charles sat in the passenger side of Victoria's convertible two-seater, watching her through the window of the dry cleaner's. He would have expected her to drive a more practical car. A sedan, or even a mini SUV. Not a sporty, candy-apple-red little number that she zipped around in at speeds matched only on the autobahn. And it had a manual transmission, which he found to be a rarity among females. Sizewise, however, it was a perfect fit. Petite and compact, just like her. So petite that his head might brush the top had he not bent down.

She was full of surprises today—the least of which was her reaction when he greeted her wearing nothing but a towel. To put it mildly, she'd been flustered. After her chilly reception last night in the office, he was beginning to wonder if she might be a bit tougher to seduce than he had first anticipated. Now he was sure that she was as good as his. Even if that meant playing dirty. Like deliberately dropping his towel before he cleared the closet door.

Victoria emerged from the building with an armload of clean clothes, wrapped in plastic and folded over one arm. She tucked them into the trunk, then slipped into the driver's seat. Her skirt rode several inches up her thighs, giving him a delicious view of her stocking-clad legs.

If she noticed him looking, she didn't let on.

"They got the stain out of your jacket sleeve," she told him, as she turned the key and the engine roared to life. She checked the rearview mirror for oncoming traffic, then jammed her foot down on the accelerator and whipped out onto the road, shifting so smoothly he barely felt the switch of the gears.

She swung around a corner and he gripped the armrest to keep from falling over. "You in a hurry?"

She shot him a bland look. "No."

She downshifted and whipped around another corner so fast he could swear the tires on one side actually lifted off the pavement.

"You know, the building isn't going anywhere," he said.

"This is the way I drive. If you don't like it, don't ask to ride with me." She took another corner at high speed, and he was pretty sure she was doing it just to annoy him.

If she drove this way all the time, it was a wonder she was still alive. "Out of curiosity, how many accidents have you been in?"

"I've never been in an accident." She whipped into the next lane, cutting off the car directly behind them, whose driver blared its horn in retaliation.

"Have you caused many?"

She shot him another one of those looks. "No."

"Next you'll try to tell me you haven't gotten a speeding ticket."

This time she stayed silent. That's what he figured.

She took a sharp left into the underground parking at his building, used her card key to open the gate, zipped into her assigned spot, and cut the engine.

"Well, that was an adventure," he said, unbuckling his seat belt.

She dropped her keys in her purse and opened her door. "I got you here alive, didn't I?"

Only by the grace of God, he was sure.

They got out and walked to the elevator, taking it up to the tenth floor. She stood silently beside him the entire time. She could never be accused of being too chatty. Since they left his house she hadn't said a word that wasn't initiated by a question. Maybe she was in a snit about the towel. She had enjoyed the free show, but didn't want to admit it.

The elevator doors opened at their floor, and as they stepped off he rested a hand on the small of her back. A natural reaction, but she didn't seem to appreciate his attempt to be a gentleman.

She jerked away and shot lasers at him with her eyes. "What are you doing?"

He held his hands up in a defensive gesture. "Sorry. Just being polite."

"Do you touch all of your female employees inappropriately?"

What was her problem? Here he thought she'd begun to warm to him, but he couldn't seem to get an accurate read on her.

"I didn't mean to offend you."

"Well, you did."

A pair standing in the hallway outside his office cut their conversation short to look at him and Victoria.

"Why don't we step into my office and talk about this," he said quietly. She nodded, then he almost made the monumental error of touching her again, drawing his hand away a second before it grazed her shoulder.

He couldn't help it; he was a physical person. And until today, no one had ever seemed to have a problem with that.

Penelope was already sitting at her desk, tapping away at her keyboard. The only hint of a reaction as he ushered Victoria to his office door was a slight lift of her left brow. He liked that about his secretary. She was always discreet. He also knew exactly what she was thinking. He'd lost another assistant already. Not all that unusual, until he factored in that he hadn't even slept with this one yet.

"Penelope, hold my calls, please." He opened the door and gestured Victoria inside, then closed it behind them. "Have a seat."

Her chin jutted out stubbornly. "I'd rather stand, thank you."

"Fine." He could see that she wasn't going to make this easy. He rounded his desk and sat down. "Now, would you like to tell me what the problem is?"

"The *problem* is that your behavior today has been completely inappropriate."

"All I did was touch your back."

"Employers are not supposed to walk around naked in front of their employees."

He leaned forward and propped his elbows on the desk. "I wasn't naked."

"Not the entire time."

So, she had been looking. "Need I point out that you were in *my* house? When I walked into *my* closet I had no reason to expect you would be there. Sniffing my shirts."

Her cheeks blushed pink, but she didn't back down. "And I suppose the towel accidentally fell off."

"Again, if you hadn't been ogling me, you wouldn't have seen anything."

Her eyes went wide with indignation. "I was not ogling you!"

"Face it, sweetheart, you couldn't keep your eyes off me." He leaned back in his chair. "In fact, I felt a little violated."

"*You* felt violated?" She clamped her jaw so tight he

worried she might crack her teeth. She wasn't easy to rile, but once he got her going…damn.

"But I'm willing to forgive and forget," he said.

"I've read your e-mails and listened to your phone messages. I know the kind of man that you are, and I'm telling you to back off. I don't want to be here any more than you want me to, but you have done such a thorough job of ruining my family that I need this position. The way I see it, we're stuck with each other. If you're trying to get me to quit, it isn't going to work. And if you continue to prance around naked in front of me and touch me inappropriately I'll slap a sexual harassment suit on you so fast you won't know what hit you."

He couldn't repress the smile that was itching to curl the corner of his mouth. "I was *prancing?*"

Her mouth fell open, as though she couldn't believe he was making a joke out of this. "You really are a piece of work."

"Thank you."

"That wasn't a compliment! You have got to be the most arrogant, self-centered—" she struggled for the right word, but all she could come up with was "—*jerk* I have ever met!"

He shrugged. "Arrogant, yes. Self-centered, occasionally. But anyone will tell you I'm a nice guy."

*"Nice?"*

"And fair."

*"Fair?* You orchestrated the deal that ruined my father. That stole from us the land that has been in our family for five generations, and you call that fair? We

lost our business and our home. We lost *everything* because of you."

He wasn't sure where she was getting her information, but she was way off. "We didn't *steal* anything. The deal we offered your father was a gift."

Her face twisted with outrage. "A *gift?*"

"He wouldn't have gotten a better deal from anyone else."

"Ruining good men in the name of the royal family doesn't make it any less sleazy or wrong."

This was all beginning to make sense now. Her lack of gratitude toward the royal family and her very generous employment contract. And there was only one explanation. "You have no idea the financial shape that the Houghton was in, do you?"

She instantly went on the defensive. "What is that supposed to mean? Yes, my father handled the financial end of the business, but he kept me informed. Business was slow, no thanks to the Royal Inn, but we were by no means sinking."

Suddenly he felt very sorry for her. And he didn't like what he was going to have to do next, but it was necessary. She deserved to know the truth, before she did something ill-advised and made a fool of both herself and her father.

He pressed the intercom on his desk. "Penelope, would you please bring in the file for the buyout on the Houghton Hotel."

"What are you doing?" Victoria demanded.

Probably making a huge mistake. "Something against my better judgment."

Victoria stood there, stiff and tight-lipped until Penelope appeared a moment later with a brown accordion file stuffed to capacity. She handed it to Charles, but not before she flashed him a swift, stern glance. Penelope knew what he was doing and the risk he was taking. And it was clear that she didn't approve. But she didn't say a word. She just walked out and shut the door behind her.

"The contents in this file are confidential," he told Victoria. "I could be putting my career in jeopardy by showing it to you. But I think it's something you need to see. In fact, I know it is."

At first he thought she might refuse to read it. For several long moments she just stared at him. But curiosity must have gotten the best of her, because finally she reached out and took the file.

"Take that into your office and look it over," he said.

Without a word she turned and walked through the door separating their offices.

"Come see me if you have questions," he called after her, just before she shut the door firmly behind her. And he was sure she would have questions. Because as far as he could tell, everything her father had told her was a lie.

# Four

Victoria felt sick.

Sick in her mind and in her heart. Sick all the way down to the center of her soul. And the more she read, the worse she felt.

She was barely a quarter of the way through the file and it was already undeniably clear that not only had the royal family not stolen anything from her and her father, they had rescued them from inevitable and total ruin.

Had they not stepped in, the bank would have foreclosed on mortgages she hadn't even been aware that her father had levied against the hotel. And he was so far behind in their property taxes, the property had been just days from being seized.

The worst part was that the trouble began when Victoria was a baby, after her grandfather passed away and her father inherited control of the hotel. All that time he'd been riding a precarious, financial roller coaster, living far above their means. Until it had finally caught up to him. And he had managed to keep it a secret by blatantly lying to her.

She had trusted him. Sacrificed so much because she thought she owed him.

Because of the royal family's generous offer, she and her father had a roof over their heads. And she had the opportunity for a career that would launch her further than she might have ever dreamed possible. Yet she still felt as though the rug had been yanked violently from under her. Everything she knew about her father and their business, *about her life,* was a lie.

And she had seen enough.

She gathered the papers and tucked them neatly back into the file. Though she dreaded facing Charles, admitting her father's deception, what choice did she have? Besides, he probably had a pretty good idea already that something in her family dynamic was amiss. If nothing else, she owed him an apology for her unfounded accusations. And a heartfelt thank-you for… well…*everything*. His family's generosity and especially their discretion.

And there was only one thing left to do. Only one thing she *could* do.

She picked up the phone and dialed Charles's extension. He answered on the first ring. "Is now a good time to speak with you?"

"Of course," he said. "Come right in."

She hung up the phone, but for several long seconds

just sat there, working up the courage to face him. And she thought yesterday had been humiliating. Getting her butt out of the chair and walking to his office, tail between her legs, was one of the hardest things she'd ever done.

Charles sat at his desk. He had every right to look smug, but he wore a sympathetic smile instead. And honestly she couldn't decide which was worse. She didn't deserve his sympathy.

She handed him the file. "Thank you for showing me this. For being honest with me."

"I thought you deserved the truth."

She took a deep breath. "First, I want to thank you and the royal family for your generosity. Please let them know how much we appreciate their intervention."

"'We'?" he asked, knowing full well that her father didn't appreciate anything the royal family had done for them.

Although for the life of her, she couldn't imagine why. Pride, she supposed. Or stubbornness. Whatever the reason, she was in no position to make excuses for him. Nor would she want to. He had gotten them into this mess, and any consequences he suffered were his own doing.

"And while I appreciate the opportunity to work for the Royal Inn," she said, removing her ID badge and setting it on his desk, "I'm afraid I won't be accepting the position."

His brow furrowed. "I don't understand."

She had taken this job only to appease her father, and now everything was different. She didn't owe him anything. For the first tine in her life she was going to make a decision based entirely on what *she* wanted.

"I'm not a charity case," she told Charles. "I owe you too much already. And unlike my father, I don't care to be indebted to anyone."

"You've seen the file, Victoria. We were under no obligation to your father. Do you honestly believe we would have hired you if we didn't feel you were qualified for the position?"

She didn't know what to believe anymore. "I'm sorry, but I just can't."

"What will you do?"

She shrugged. She was in hotel management, and the Royal Inn was the biggest game on the island. She would never find a position with comparable pay anywhere else. Not on Morgan Isle, anyway. That could mean a move off the island. Maybe it was time for a change, time to stop leaning on her father and be truly independent for the first time in her life. Or maybe it was he who had been leaning on her.

"I'll find another job," she said.

"What will you do until then?"

She honestly didn't know. Since the buyout, what savings she'd had were quickly vanishing. If she went much longer without a paycheck, she would be living on the streets.

"I have an idea," Charles said. "A mutually beneficial arrangement."

She wasn't sure she liked the sound of that, but the least she could do was hear him out. She folded her arms and said, "I'm listening."

"You've seen the shambles my life is in. Stay, just long enough to get things back in order and to hire and train a new assistant, and when you go, you'll leave with a letter of recommendation so impressive that anyone would be a fool not to hire you."

It was tempting, but she already owed him too much. This was something she needed to do on her own.

She shook her head. "You've done too much already."

He leaned forward in his seat. "*You* would be the one doing *me* the favor. I honestly don't have the time to train someone else."

"I've been here *two* days. Technically someone should be training me."

"You're a fast learner." When she didn't answer he leaned forward and said, "Victoria, I'm desperate."

He did look a little desperate, but she couldn't escape the feeling that he was doing it just to be nice. Which shouldn't have been a bad thing. And she should have been jumping at his offer, but she couldn't escape the feeling that she didn't deserve his sympathy.

"Do this one thing for me," he coaxed, "and we'll call it even. You won't owe me and I won't owe you."

She would have loved nothing more than to put this entire awful experience behind her and start fresh.

"I would have to insist you pay me only an assistant's wage," she said.

He looked surprised. "That's not much."

"Maybe, but it's fair."

"Fine," he agreed. "If that's what you want."

"How long would I have to stay?" she asked.

"How about two months."

Yeah, right. "How about one *week?*"

He narrowed his eyes at her. "Six weeks."

"Two weeks," she countered.

"Four."

*"Three."*

"Deal," he said with a grin.

She took a deep breath and blew it out. Three weeks working with the duke. It was longer than she was comfortable with, but at the very least it would give her time to look for another job. She had interviewed hundreds of people in her years at the Houghton, yet she had never so much as put together a résumé for herself. Much less had to look for employment. She barely knew where to begin.

"I'll have Penelope post an ad for the assistant's position. I'll leave it to you to interview the applicants. Then, of course, they'll have to meet my approval."

"Of course."

"Why don't we catch an early lunch today and discuss exactly what it is I'm looking for?" His smile said business was the last thing on his mind.

Were they back to that again?

If she was going to survive the next three weeks working for him, she was going to have to set some boundaries. Establish parameters.

"I'm not going to sleep with you," she said.

If her direct approach surprised him, he didn't let it show. He just raised one brow slightly higher than the other. "I don't know how you did things at the Houghton, but here, *lunch* isn't code for sex."

On the contrary, that's exactly what it was. Practically everything he said was a double entendre. "I'm not a member of your harem."

One corner of his mouth tipped up. "I have a harem?"

Was he forgetting that she'd listened to his phone messages? "I just thought I should make it clear up front. Because you seem to believe you're God's gift to the female race."

He shot her a very contrived stunned look. "You mean I'm *not?*"

"I'm sorry to say, I don't find you the least bit attractive." It was kind of a lie. Physically she found him incredibly attractive. His personality, on the other hand, needed serious work.

He shrugged. "If you say so."

He was baiting her, but she wouldn't give him the satisfaction of a response. "Have a list of employment requirements to me by end of day and I'll see that the ad is placed." She already had a pretty good idea of the sort of employee he was looking for. More emphasis on looks than intelligence or capability. But she was going to find him an assistant who could actually do the job. And she would hopefully be doing it sooner than three weeks. The faster she got out of here, the better.

"You'll have it by five," he said.

"Thank you. I should get back to work." She still had a backload of e-mail and phone messages to sort through.

She was almost to her office when he called her name, and something in his voice said he was up to no good. She sighed quietly to herself, and with her hand on the doorknob, turned back to him. Ready for a fight. "Yes?"

"Thank you."

"For what?" she asked, expecting some sort of snappy, sarcastic comeback or a sexually charged innuendo.

Instead, he just said, "For sticking around."

She was so surprised, all she could do was nod as she opened the door and slipped into her office. The really weird thing was, she was pretty sure he genuinely meant it. And it touched her somewhere deep down.

If she wasn't careful, she just might forget how much she didn't like him.

It was almost four-thirty when Charles popped his head into her office and handed Victoria the list of employment requirements. And early, no less.

"Are you busy?" he asked.

What now? Wasn't it a bit early for a dinner invitation? "Why?"

"You up for a field trip?"

She set the list in her urgent to-do pile. "I guess that all depends on where you want to go." If it was a field trip to his bedroom, then no, she would pass.

"I have a meeting at the palace in half an hour. I thought you might want to tag along. It would be a chance for you to learn the ropes."

A tickle of excitement worked its way up from her belly. Anyone who lived on Morgan Isle dreamed of going to the palace and meeting the royal family.

But honestly, what was the point? "Why bother? I'll only be working for you for three weeks."

"Yes, but how will you train your replacement if you don't learn the job first?"

He had a point. Although his logic was a little

backward. But the truth was, she really *wanted* to go. After all, when would she ever get an opportunity like this one again?

"When you put it that way," she said, pushing away from her desk, "I suppose I should."

"A car is waiting for us downstairs."

She grabbed her purse from the bottom desk drawer and her sweater from the hook on the back of the door, then followed him through the outer office past Penelope—who didn't even raise her head to acknowledge them—to the elevator. He was uncharacteristically quiet as they rode down and he led her through the lobby to the shiny, black, official-looking Bentley parked out front. Not that she knew him all that well, but he always seemed to have something to say. Too much, usually.

They settled in the leather-clad backseat, and the driver pulled out into traffic. She wasn't typically the chatty type, but she felt this irrational, uncontrollable urge to fill the silence. Maybe because as long as they were talking, she didn't have to think about the overpowering sense of his presence beside her. He was so large, filled his side of the seat so thoroughly, she felt almost crowded against the door. It would take only the slightest movement to cause their knees to bump. And the idea of any sort of contact in the privacy of the car, even accidental, made her pulse jump.

When she couldn't stand the silence another second, she heard herself ask, "Not looking forward to this meeting?"

The sound of her voice startled him, as though he'd forgotten he wasn't alone. "Why do you ask?"

"You seem…preoccupied."

"Do I?"

"You haven't made a single suggestive or inappropriate comment since we left your office."

He laughed and said, "No, I'm not looking forward to it. Delivering bad news is never pleasant."

He didn't elaborate, and though she was dying of curiosity, she didn't ask. It was none of her business. And honestly, the less she knew about the royal family's business, the better.

The drive to the palace was a short one. As the gates came into view, Victoria's heart did a quick shimmy in her chest. She was really going to visit the royal palace. Where kings and queens had lived for generations, and heads of state regularly visited. Though she had lived on Morgan Isle her entire life, not ten miles from the palace, she never imagined she would ever step foot within its walls. Or come face-to-face with the royal family.

Charles leaned forward and told the driver. "Take us to the front doors." He turned to Victoria. "Normally you would use the business entrance in the back, but I thought for your first visit you should get the royal treatment."

The car rolled to a stop, and royally clothed footmen posted on either side of the enormous double doors descended the stairs. One opened the car door and offered a hand encased in pristine white cotton to help her out. It was oddly surreal. She'd never put much stock in fairy tales, but standing at the foot of the palace steps, she felt a little like Cinderella. Only she wasn't there for a ball. And even if she were, there were no single princes in residence to fall in love with her. Just an arrogant, womanizing duke.

Which sounded more like a nightmare than any fairy tale she'd ever read.

She and Charles climbed the stairs, and as they approached the top the gilded doors swung open, welcoming them inside.

Walking into the palace, through the cavernous foyer, was like stepping into a different world. An alternate reality where everything was rich and elegant and larger than life. She had never seen so much marble, gold, and velvet, yet it was tastefully proportioned so as not to appear gaudy. She turned in a circle, her heels clicking against marble buffed to a gleaming shine, taking in the antique furnishings, the vaulted and ornately painted ceilings.

Though she had seen it many times in photos and on television documentaries, and on television documentaries, those were substitute for the real thing.

"What do you think?" Charles asked.

"It's amazing," she breathed. "Does everyone who visits get this kind of welcome?"

"Not exactly. But I feel as though everyone should experience the entire royal treatment at least one time. Don't you think?"

She nodded, although she couldn't help wondering if he had done this out of the kindness of his heart or if instead he had ulterior motives. She knew from experience that men like him often did. How many other women had he brought here, hoping to impress them with his royalty? Not that she considered herself one of his *women*. But he very well might. In fact, she was pretty sure he did. Men like him objectified women, saw them as nothing more than playthings.

And she was buying into it. Playing right into his hand. Shame on her for letting down her guard.

She put a chokehold on her excitement and flashed him a passive smile. "Well, thank you. It was a nice surprise."

"Would you like to meet the family?" he asked.

Her heart leapt up into her throat. "The f-family?"

"We have a meeting scheduled, so they should all be together in the king's suite."

The *entire* family? All at once? And he said it so casually, as if meeting royalty was a daily occurrence for her.

But what was she going to tell him? *No?*

"If it's not a problem," she said, although she didn't have the first clue what she would say to them.

"They're expecting us."

Expecting them?

She went from being marginally nervous to shaking in her pumps.

He stepped forward, toward the stairs, but she didn't budge. She couldn't. She felt frozen in place, as though her shoes had melted into the marble.

He stopped and looked back at her. "You coming?"

She nodded, but she couldn't seem to get her feet to move. She just stood there like an idiot.

Charles brow furrowed a little. "You okay?"

"Of course." If she ignored the fact that her legs wouldn't work and that a nest of nerves the size of a boulder weighed heavy in her gut.

A grin curled one corner of his mouth. "A little nervous, maybe?"

"Maybe," she conceded. "A little."

"You have nothing to worry about. They don't bite." He paused then added, "Much."

She shot him a look.

He grinned and said, "I'm kidding. They're looking forward to meeting you." He jerked his head in the direction of the stairs. "Come on."

She didn't pitch a fit this time when Charles touched a hand to the small of her back to give her a gentle shove in the right direction. But he kept his hands to himself as he led her up the marble staircase to the second floor, gesturing to points of interest along the way. Family portraits dating back centuries, priceless heirlooms and gifts from foreign visitors and dignitaries.

It all sounded a bit rehearsed to her, but the truth was, as the family lawyer, he'd probably taken lots of people on a similar tour. Not just women he was hoping to impress. And it did take her mind off of her nerves.

"The family residence is this way," he said, leading her toward a set of doors guarded by two very large, frightening-looking security officers. He gestured to the wing across the hall. "The guest suites are down that way."

Feeling like an interloper, she followed him toward the residence. The guards stepped forward as they approached, and Victoria half-expected them to tackle her before she could make it through the doors. But instead they opened the doors and stepped aside so she and Charles could pass. Inside was a long, wide, quiet hallway and at least a dozen sets of double doors.

Behind one of those doors, she thought, waited the entire royal family. And what she hadn't even considered until just now was that each and every one of them knew the dire financial situation she and her father had been in. For all she knew, they might believe she was responsible. She could only hope that Charles had told them the truth.

"Ready?" he asked.

Ready? How did one prepare herself for a moment like this? But she took a deep breath and blew it out, then looked up at Charles and said, "Let's do it."

# Five

Victoria was tough, Charles would give her that.

Typically when people were introduced to members of the royal family, it was one or two at a time. Victoria was meeting King Phillip and Queen Hannah; Prince Ethan and his wife, Lizzy; and Princess Sophie and her fiancé, Alex, all at the same time.

Everyone was gathered in the sitting room of Hannah and Phillip's suite, and they all rose from their seats when he and Victoria entered.

If she was nervous, it didn't show. Her curtsy was flawless, and when she spoke her voice was clear and steady. It never failed to intrigue him how a woman so seemingly small and unassuming could dominate a room with sheer confidence. He could see that everyone was impressed. And though it was totally irrational, he felt proud of her. Hiring her had in no way been his idea. He had merely been following orders.

After the introductions and several minutes of polite small talk, an aide was called in to give Victoria a tour of the business offices and familiarize her with palace procedure.

"I like her," Sophie said, the instant they were gone. It had been at her insistence that they had hired Victoria in the first place.

Charles nodded. "She's very capable."

"And attractive," Ethan noted, which got him a playful elbow jab in the side from his very pregnant wife, Lizzy.

"Stunning," Hannah added.

"Quite," Charles agreed. "And she would have been an asset to the Royal Inn."

"Would have been?" Phillip asked.

Sophie narrowed her eyes at Charles. "What did you do?"

"Nothing!" He held both hands up defensively. "I swear."

He explained Victoria's outburst and admitted to showing her the file on the Houghton sale. "She seems to think we see her as some sort of charity case. She has no idea her expertise. Nor does she have the slightest clue how valuable she is. Had it not been for her, I think the Houghton would have collapsed years ago."

"Then it will be up to you to see that she learns her value," Phillip said.

Easier said than done when she was suspicious of his every move. "She's stubborn as hell. But I'm sure I can convince her."

"Stubborn as hell," Alex said, glancing over at Princess Sophie. "She'll fit right in, won't she?"

Now she narrowed her eyes at him. "Is it so wrong that I don't want my wedding to be a spectacle? That I prefer small and intimate?"

"You have other news for us?" Phillip asked Charles, forestalling another potential wedding argument.

Yes, it was time they got to it. Charles took a seat on the couch beside Sophie, rubbing his palms together.

"I gather the news isn't good," Ethan said.

"The DNA test confirmed it. She's the real deal," Charles told them. "Melissa Thornsby is your illegitimate sister and heir to the throne."

"We have a sister," Sophie said, as though trying out the sound of it. Phillip and Hannah remained quietly concerned.

"And here I believed I had the distinction of being the only illegitimate heir to the throne," Ethan quipped, even though he was the one who had taken the time to investigate their father's notorious reputation with women, and the possibility of more illegitimate children. But who could have imagined that King Frederick would have been so bold as to not only have an affair with the former prime minister's wife but to father a child with her? And he never told a soul. Had Ethan not stumbled across a file of newspaper clippings King Frederick had left hidden after his death, they might never have learned the truth.

"She's older than Phillip?" Lizzy asked.

"Twenty-three days," Charles said.

Everyone exchanged worried glances, but Hannah

broached the subject no one else seemed willing to speak aloud. "Could she take the crown?"

This was the part Charles hadn't been looking forward to. "Technically? Yes, she could. Half Royal or not, she's the oldest."

Hannah frowned. "But she wasn't even raised here."

"She was born here, though. She's still considered a citizen."

In an uncustomary show of emotion, Phillip cursed under his breath. Losing the crown for him wouldn't be an issue of status or power. Phillip truly loved his country and had devoted his entire life in the preparation to become its leader. To lose that would devastate him. "We'll fight it," he said.

"I don't think it will come to that," Charles said. "She doesn't seem the type to take on the role as the leader of a country. Despite a first-rate education, other than heading up a host of charities, she's never had a career."

"As a proper princess wouldn't," Phillip said, sounding cautiously optimistic. "Meaning she could very well fit right in."

"Would she be the type to go after our money?" Sophie asked.

Charles shook his head. "I seriously doubt it."

"Why?"

"Because she has almost as much money as you do. She inherited a considerable trust from her parents on her twenty-first birthday, and her aunt and uncle left her a fortune. She's at the top of the food chain in New Orleans high society."

"How did she take the news?" Hannah asked.

"According to the attorney, it was definitely a shock, but she's eager to meet everyone. So much so that she's dropping everything so that she can move here. Temporarily at first. Then she'll decide if she wants to stay."

"Her place is here with her family," Sophie said.

"We can't force her to stay," Lizzy pointed out.

"True," Hannah said, looking pointedly at Phillip. "But if we make her feel welcome she'll be more inclined to."

It was no secret that when Ethan joined the family, Phillip had been less than welcoming to his half brother. But in Phillip's defense, Ethan had gone out of his way to be difficult. Since then, they had put their differences aside and now behaved like brothers. Not that they didn't occasionally butt heads.

"When will she come?" Phillip asked.

"Saturday."

"We'll need to see that a suite is prepared," Sophie said. "I suggest housing her in the guest suite at first, with restricted privileges to the residence."

"I agree," Phillip said. "Lizzy, can you please handle the details?"

Lizzy nodded eagerly. Going from full-time employment to royal status had been rough for her. And despite a somewhat trying pregnancy, she was always looking for tasks to keep her busy until the baby arrived. "I'll take care of it immediately."

Phillip turned to Sophie, who handled media relations. "We'll have to issue a press release immediately. I don't want to see a story in the tabloids before we make a formal announcement."

Sophie nodded. "I'll see that it's done today."

"Speaking of the tabloids," Alex said, "you know they're going to be all over this. And all over her." Having recently been a target of the media himself when his ex-wife fed them false information about his relationship with the princess, he knew how vicious they could be.

"She'll be instructed on exactly what she should and shouldn't say," Charles assured him. "Although given her position in society, I don't think handling the press will be an issue."

"I'd like to keep this low-key," Phillip said, then he rose from his seat, signaling the end of the meeting. "Keep us posted."

Hannah tugged on his sleeve. "Are you forgetting something, Your Highness?"

He looked down at his wife and smiled. "You're sure you want to do this now?"

She nodded.

He touched her cheek affectionately, then announced, with distinct happiness and pride, "Hannah is pregnant."

Everyone seemed as stunned as they were excited.

Sophie laughed and said, "My gosh! You two certainly didn't waste any time. Frederick is barely three months old!"

Hannah blushed. "It wasn't planned, and I only just found out this morning. We'd like to keep it quiet until closer to the end of my first trimester. But I was too excited not to tell the family."

"I think it's wonderful," Lizzy said, a hand on her

own rounded belly. She shot Sophie a meaningful glance. "At this rate we'll have the palace filled with children in no time."

Sophie emphatically shook her head. "Not from me you won't. Alex and I have already discussed it and decided to wait until he's not traveling back and forth to the States so much."

"You say that now," Lizzy teased. "Things have a way of not working out as you plan."

She would know. Her pregnancy had been an unplanned surprise. She'd gone from palace employee to royal family member with one hasty but genuinely happy *I do*.

"What about Charles?" Sophie said, flashing him a wry grin. "He's not even married yet. Why not pick on him?"

"When it comes to marriage," Phillip said, sounding only slightly exasperated, "*yet* is not a word in Charles's vocabulary."

Phillip was absolutely right. And this was not a conversation Charles cared to have any part of. The last thing he needed was the entire family meddling in his love life.

"Wow," he said, glancing down at his watch. "Would you look at the time. I should be going."

"What's the matter, Charles?" Sophie asked. "Have you got a hot date?"

In fact he did. Even though the "date" in question didn't know it yet.

Phillip just grinned. "If you hear anything else from Melissa or her attorney, you'll let us know?"

"Of course." He said the obligatory goodbyes, then

made a hasty retreat out into the hall. Before he could escape the residence, Ethan called after him.

"Charles, hold up a minute." He wore a concerned expression, which was enough to cause Charles concern himself. Ethan was one of the most easygoing people he knew.

"Is there a problem?" he asked.

Ethan paused for a moment, then sighed and shook his head. "I guess there's really no tactful way to say this, so I'm just going to say it. The family is asking, as a personal favor, that you not have an affair with Victoria."

For an instant, Charles was too stunned to speak. Then all he could manage was "I beg your pardon?"

"You heard me."

Yes, he had. But he must have been mistaken. He'd devoted his life to his family, true, but that didn't give them the right to dictate who he could or couldn't sleep with. "What are you suggesting, Ethan?"

Ethan lowered his voice. "I don't have to *suggest* anything. It's common knowledge that the employees you sleep with don't last. Normally that isn't a problem because they're *your* personal employees, and how you run your firm is your own business. But Victoria is an employee of the royal family, as are you, and as such, policy states there can be no personal relationship. If we can convince her to stay, her expertise will be a great asset to the Royal Inn. That isn't likely to happen if you and she become…*intimately* involved."

"That's a little hypocritical coming from you," Charles said. "Seeing as how you knocked up a palace employee."

It was a cheap shot, but the arrow hit its mark.

Ethan's expression darkened. "Make no mistake Charles, this is something the *entire* family is asking. Not just me."

And what if Charles said no? What if he slept with her and she refused to stay? Would he be ousted as the family attorney? "This sounds a bit like a threat to me."

"It's nothing more than a request."

Though only a cousin, Charles had always been an integral part of the royal family. For the first time in his life he felt like an outsider.

And he didn't like it.

"Do whatever it takes to make her stay," Ethan said, and there was a finality to his words that set Charles even deeper on edge.

"I need to go fetch my assistant," Charles told him, then he turned and left before he said something he might later regret.

He found Victoria in the main business office with one of the secretaries. For the life of him he couldn't remember her name. She was explaining the phone and security system to Victoria. As he approached they both looked up at him.

"Finished already?" Victoria asked.

Charles nodded. "Ready to go?"

"Sure." She thanked the secretary, whose name still escaped him, grabbed her purse, and followed Charles out. She practically had to jog to keep up with his brisk, longer stride. He led her out the back way this time, where she would come and go should the position ever call for her coming back to the palace.

"Meeting not go well?" she asked from behind him, as they passed the kitchen.

"What makes you think that?"

"You're awfully quiet. And you seem to be in a terrible rush to leave," she said, sounding a touch winded.

He made an effort to slow his pace. It wasn't the meeting itself that was troubling him. That had gone rather well, all things considered. "It was fine," he said.

The car was waiting for them when they stepped out of the back entrance. They got in, and he almost directed the driver to take them back to the office, but then he remembered that he was treating Victoria to dinner.

Instead he told him, "The Royal Inn."

"Why are we going to the Royal Inn?" she asked.

"I'm taking you to Les Régal De Rois for dinner," he said. He expected an argument or an immediate refusal. Instead she just looked amused, which rubbed his already frayed nerves.

"Is that an invitation?" she asked.

"No. Just a fact."

"Really?"

He nodded. "Yep."

"What about my car?"

"It'll be fine in the parking garage overnight. I'll arrange for my car to pick you up in the morning."

She mulled that over, looking skeptical. He steeled himself for the inevitable argument. In fact, he was looking forward to it. He needed a target to vent a little steam. Even though he was supposed to be convincing her to stay, not using her for target practice.

Instead she said, "Okay."

"Okay?"

"I'll go to dinner with you, but only if I get to choose the restaurant."

He shrugged. "All right."

"And you have to let me pay."

Absolutely not. He never let women pay. It had been hammered into him from birth that it was a man's duty— his *responsibility*—to pick up the check. As far as his mother was concerned, chivalry was alive and kicking.

"Considering your current employment status, it might be wise to let me cover it," he said.

She folded her arms across her chest. "Let me worry about that."

Would it hurt to let her *think* she was paying? But when it came time to get the bill, he would take it. It's not as if she would wrestle it out of his hand. At least, he didn't think she would. She may have been independent, but he knew from experience that deep down, all women loved to be pampered. They liked when men held doors and paid the check. Expected it, even.

"Fine," he agreed.

She leaned forward and instructed the driver to take them to an unfamiliar address in the bay area. For all he knew she could be taking him to a fast-food establishment.

The driver looked to Charles for confirmation, and he nodded.

What the heck. He was always up for an adventure.

# Six

It wasn't a fast food restaurant.

It was a cozy, moderately priced bistro tucked between two upscale women's clothing stores in the shopping district. The maître d' greeted Victoria warmly and Charles with the proper fuss afforded royalty, then seated them at a table in a secluded corner. It was quiet and intimate and soaked in the flickering glow of warm candlelight. Their waiter appeared instantly to take their drink orders—a white wine for Victoria and a double scotch for him—then he listed the specials for the evening.

"I recommend the prime rib," Victoria said, once he was gone.

Charles drew the line at letting his date order for him, and he used the term *date* very loosely. Besides, his encounter with Ethan had pretty much killed his appetite.

"I take it you come here often," he said.

"I love this place," Victoria said with a smile. An honest to goodness, genuine smile. And the force of it was so devastating it nearly knocked him backward out of his chair. She might not have smiled often, but it was certainly worth the wait.

The waiter reappeared only seconds later with their drinks. Charles took a deep slug of scotch, relishing the smooth burn as it slid down his throat and spread heat through his stomach. Three or four more of these and he would be right as rain, but he'd never been one to find solace in a bottle.

Victoria took a sip of her wine, watching him curiously. "Would you like to talk about it?"

"Talk about what?"

"Whatever it is that's bothering you." She propped her elbow on the table, dropped her chin in her hand, and gazed across the candlelight at him, her eyes warm, her features soft in the low light.

She really was stunning. And not at all the sort of woman he was typically attracted to. But maybe that was the appeal. Maybe he was tired of the same old thing. Maybe he needed to spice things up a bit.

The family had put the kibosh on that, though, hadn't they? And since when did he ever let anyone tell him whom he could or couldn't pursue?

"What makes you think something is bothering me?"

"That's why I agreed to dinner," she said. "You looked as though you needed a sympathetic ear."

She certainly looked sympathetic, which for some reason surprised him. He never imagined her having a soft side. But he wasn't one to air his troubles. Although, would it hurt to play the pity card this one time? And maybe, in the process, do his job and convince Victoria to stay with the hotel?

He pulled in a deep, contemplative breath, then blew it out. "Family issues," he said, keeping it cryptic. Baiting her. But if he expected her to try to drag it out of him, boy, had he been wrong.

She just sat there sipping her wine, waiting for him to continue.

He dropped another crumb. "Suffice it to say that the family wasn't happy to hear that you're not staying with the Royal Inn."

"I'm sorry to hear that."

"I've been instructed to do whatever it takes to convince you to stay."

If she was flattered, it didn't show on her face. "But that isn't what's bothering you," she said.

Who was baiting whom here?

Though he'd had no intention of telling her what was really said, he supposed that if anyone could understand a backstabbing, meddling family, it was her.

"I've been asked by the family not to pursue you socially."

A grin tipped up the corners of her mouth. "In other words, don't sleep with me."

Her candor surprised him a little, but then, what did she have to lose? This was only a temporary position for her. "That was the gist of it, yes."

"And that upsets you?"

"Wouldn't it upset you?"

"I suppose. But then, I don't have a notorious reputation for sleeping with my employees."

He couldn't help but wonder where she'd heard that. "According to whom?"

"The girls in the palace office talk."

He couldn't exactly deny it, but still he felt... offended. Whom he dated was no one's concern. Especially the girls in the office. "What else did the *girls* have to say about me?"

"Are you sure you want to know?"

Did he? Did it even matter? When had he ever cared what people thought of him?

But curiosity got the best of him. "I'm a big boy. I think I can handle it."

"They told me that your assistants never last more than a few weeks."

Again, he couldn't deny it. But that was just the nature of business. Assistants' positions notoriously had a high turnover rate. Most were overworked and underpaid.

Were the girls in the office taking that into account?

Not to say that he was an unfair employer. But he didn't owe anyone an explanation.

"And I'm not your usual type."

"I have a type?"

"Tall, leggy, impressed by your power and position."

Could he help that people were impressed by his title?

"Oh, and they told me that you objectify women," she added. "But I already knew that."

Wait, what? He *objectified* women? "No, I don't."

She looked a little surprised by his denial. "Yes, you do."

"I have nothing but respect for women. I *love* women."

"Maybe that's part of the problem."

"What the hell is that supposed to mean?" And why did he even care what she thought of him?

"This is upsetting you," she said. "Maybe we should just drop it."

"No. I want to know how it is that I objectify women."

She studied him for a minute, then asked, "How many different women have you dated in the last month?"

"What does that have to do with anything?"

"Humor me."

"Eight or ten, maybe." Maybe more. In fact, if he counted the casual encounters in bars or clubs that led back to his bedroom, that number was probably closer to fifteen. But that didn't mean anything. Wanting to play the field, not wanting to settle down yet, did not equate into disrespect for the opposite sex.

"What were their names?" she asked.

That one stopped him. "What do you mean?"

"Their names. The women you dated. They had names, right?"

"Of course."

"So, what were they?"

He frowned. That was a lot of names. Faces he could remember, or body types. Hair color, even eye color. Names he wasn't so good with.

"I'll make it easy for you. Of the last twenty girls you dated, give me *three* names," she said.

Three names? What about the blonde from the bar last week. The bank teller with the large and plunging… portfolio. It was something simple. A *J* name. Jenny, Julie, Jeri. Or maybe it was Sara.

He was usually pretty good under pressure, but now he was drawing a blank.

"You can't do it, can you?" Victoria said, looking pleased with herself. "Here's an easy one. How about your last assistant? What was her name?"

Now this one he knew. Tall, brunette. Low, sultry voice…

It was right there, on the tip of his tongue.

"Oh, come on," she said. "Even I know this."

He took a guess, which he knew was probably a bad idea. "Diane."

"Her name was Rebecca."

"Well, she looked like a Diane to me." Mostly he'd just called her honey, or sweetheart, so he wouldn't *have* to remember her name. Because after a while they all just sort of bled together. But that didn't mean anything.

She shook her head. "That's really sad."

"So I'm not great with names. So what?"

"Name the last five male clients you met with."

They popped into his head in quick succession. One after the other, clear as if he'd read them on a list. And though he said nothing, she could read it in his expression.

The smile that followed was a smug one. "Easier, isn't it?"

He folded his arms across his chest, not liking the direction this was taking. "What's your point?"

"You remember the men because you respect them. You see them as equals. Women on the other hand exist only for your own personal amusement. They're playthings."

Though his first reaction was to deny the accusation, it *was* an interesting…hypothesis. And one he had no desire to contemplate at that particular moment, or with her.

He downed the last of his drink and signaled the waiter for the check. "We should go."

"We haven't eaten yet."

"I have to get an early start in the morning."

Her smug smile grew, as though she was feeding off his discomfort. To make matters worse, before he could take the bill from the waiter, she snatched it up. "My treat, remember?"

There didn't seem much point in arguing. And since it was only drinks, he would let her have her way this once.

She paid in cash, leaving a generous tip considering they hadn't even eaten, then they rose from their chairs and walked in silence to the door. The car was already waiting for them out front.

"I'll see you tomorrow," she said.

"You don't want a ride?"

She shook her head. "No, thanks."

"It's quite chilly."

"I'm just a few blocks from here. I could use the fresh air."

"I'll walk you," he said, because God forbid she would also accuse him of not being a gentleman.

"No, I'm fine," she said, with a smile. "But I appreciate the offer."

There was something very different about her tonight. He'd never seen her so relaxed. So pleasant and…happy.

At his expense, no doubt.

"See you tomorrow at the office." She turned to

walk away, but made it only a step or two before she stopped and turned back. "By the way, have you decided what to do?"

"What do you mean?"

"Your family? Not pursuing me. Will you listen to them?"

Good question. And despite all the hemming and hawing and claims that no one could tell him who he could or couldn't see, he had an obligation to the family. Ultimately, there was really only one clear-cut answer.

He shrugged. "I don't really have much choice."

"Well, in that case…"

Another one of those grins curled her mouth. Playful, bordering on devious, and he had the distinct impression that she was up to no good.

She stepped closer, closing the gap between them, then reached up with one hand and gripped his tie. She gave it a firm tug, and he had no choice but to lean over—it was that or asphyxiation. And when he did, she rose up on her toes and kissed him. A tender, teasing brush of her lips against his own.

Before he could react, before he could cup the back of her head and draw her in for more, it was over. She had already let go of his tie and backed away. His lips burned with the need to kiss her again. His hands ached to touch her.

He wanted her.

"What was that for?" he asked.

She shrugged, as though she accosted men on the street on a regular basis. "Just thought you should know what you're missing."

* * *

Victoria knew that kissing Charles was a really bad idea, but he had looked so adorably bewildered by their conversation in the restaurant, so hopelessly confused, she hadn't been able to resist. She thought it would be fun to mess with his head, knock him a little further off base. But what she hadn't counted on, what she hadn't anticipated, was the way it would make *her* feel.

She'd kissed her share of men before, but she felt as though, for the first time in her life, she had *really* kissed a man. It was as if a switch in her brain had been flipped and everything in her being was saying, *He's the one*.

Which was as ridiculous as it was disturbing.

Yet her legs were so wobbly and her head so dizzy that once she'd rounded the corner and was out of sight, she collapsed on a bench to collect herself.

What was wrong with her? It was just a kiss. And barely even that. So why the weak knees? The frantically beating heart and breathless feeling? Why the tingling burn in her breasts and between her thighs?

Maybe that was just the effect he had on females, something chemical, or physiological. Maybe that was why he dated so many women. They genuinely couldn't resist him.

That was probably it, she assured herself. Pheromones or hormones or something. And the effect was bound to wear off. Eventually she would even grow immune to it altogether.

She just hoped to God that he hadn't noticed. That before she let go he hadn't felt her hands shaking, that he hadn't seen her pulse throbbing at the base of her throat or the heat burning her cheeks. That he hadn't heard the waver in her voice before she turned and walked away. If he knew what he did to her, he could potentially make her life—the next few weeks, anyway—a living hell.

When she felt steady enough, she walked the two blocks to her flat. She unlocked the outer door and headed up the stairs to the third floor. The building was clean and well tended, but the flat itself was only a fraction the size of her suite at the family estate.

She stepped inside and tossed her keys and purse on the table by the door. It would be roomier once she emptied all of the boxes still sitting packed in every room. But her heart just wasn't in it. It didn't feel like home.

The light on her answering machine was flashing furiously. She checked the caller ID and saw that every one that day was from her father. He was probably eager to talk to her about the royal family, tell her more lies to cover his own mistakes.

Well, she wasn't ready to talk to him. The sting of his betrayal was too fresh. She would end up saying something she would later regret.

She erased the messages without listening to them and turned off the ringer on her phone. At times like this she wished she had a best girlfriend to confide in. Even a casual friend. Only now, with her career in the toilet, was she beginning to realize what she'd missed out on when she made the decision to devote herself entirely to her career. For the first time in her life she truly felt alone. And when she thought of her father's betrayal, the feeling intensified, sitting like a stone in her belly.

All those years of dedication and hard work, and what had it gotten her? Thanks to her father, she had lost nearly everything.

But was it fair to blame it all on him? Didn't she shoulder at least a little bit of the blame? Had she allowed it to happen by not questioning his handling of the finances? By not checking the books for herself?

By trusting him?

But what reason had he given her not to?

She shook her head and rubbed at the ache starting in her temples. Self-pity would get her nowhere. She needed to get over it, pick up the pieces, and get on with her life. And the first thing on her agenda: finding Charles a new assistant and finding herself a new job. Despite their desire to keep her in their employment, she would never feel comfortable working for the royal family. She couldn't shake the idea that their job offer had nothing to do with skill, that they had hired her out of pity.

She would never feel as though she truly fit in.

First thing in the morning she would place an ad for the assistant's position and phone her contacts at the various employment agencies in the bay area. In no time she would have Phillip a new assistant. A *capable* assistant.

And until then, she would stay as far from Charles as humanly possible.

# Seven

So much for keeping her distance from Charles.

As promised, he sent his car to fetch Victoria before work the next morning. When she heard the knock at her flat door, she just assumed it was the driver coming up to get her. But when she opened the door, Charles stood there.

He leaned casually against the doorjamb, looking attractive and fit in a charcoal pinstripe suit, a grin on his face. And not a trace of the ill ease he'd worn like a shroud the night before.

"Good morning," he said, then added, *"Victoria."*

*Okay.* "Good morning…Charles."

"I thought you would be impressed. I remembered your name."

He'd apparently taken what she said to heart. She

was genuinely and pleasantly surprised. It didn't last long, though.

"I'd say that I deserve a reward," he said, with an exaggerated wiggle of his brows.

The man was a shameless flirt, and though she hated to admit it, his teasing and innuendo wasn't nearly as offensive as it used to be.

And to be fair, he had remembered her name right from the start. Which meant nothing when she considered that she and her father were the topic of many a conversation prior to her employment with him. Of course he would remember her.

*You're rationalizing, Vic.*

The best response was no response at all.

"I just need to grab my jacket," she said. "Wait right here."

She dashed off to her bedroom, grabbed her suit jacket, and slipped it on. She was gone less than a minute, but when she returned to the door, it was closed and he wasn't there.

Had he gone back to the car?

"Nice view," she heard him say, and turned to find him standing in her cluttered living room gazing out the window.

He was *in* her flat.

The fact that it was in total disarray notwithstanding, he was just so *there*. Such a distinct and overpowering presence in a room that until that very moment had always felt open and spacious. Now they might as well have been locked in a closet together for the lack of breathing room.

*Just relax. This is not as bad as it seems. You're completely overreacting.*

She folded her arms across her chest, doing her best to sound more annoyed than nervous. "You don't take direction well, do you?"

He turned to her and smiled, and she felt it like a sucker punch to her belly. The worst part was that she was pretty sure he knew exactly what that smile was doing to her. And he had intended exactly that.

*You just had to kiss him, didn't you?*

He gestured out the window. "You have an ocean view."

Barely. Only a few snippets of blue through the buildings across the road. Nothing like the view from his home. Although it was looking decidedly more pleasing with him standing there.

Ugh. She really had to stop these random, destructive thoughts.

"I don't recall inviting you inside," she said.

"Yeah, you might want to work on those manners."

She shook her head. "God, you're arrogant."

He just grinned and gestured to the city street below. "How do you like living in the heart of the city?"

It was different. Her father's estate, *their* estate, had been in a rural setting, but she'd spent the majority of her time working in the city. A home in the bay area seemed the logical choice. "It's…convenient. Besides, I needed a change of pace. A place that didn't remind me of everything I've lost."

She cringed inwardly. Why had she told him that? It was too personal. Too private. She didn't want him getting the idea that she liked him. She didn't want to *like* him.

He nodded thoughtfully. "And how is that working out for you?"

Lousy, but he probably already figured that out.

"I'm ready to go." She walked to the door, grabbing her keys and purse from the table.

He didn't follow her. He just stood there, grinning, as though he knew something she didn't. "What's the rush?" he asked.

She looked at her watch. "It's eight-twenty."

He shrugged. "So?"

"Isn't the car waiting?"

"It's not going anywhere without us."

She didn't like the way he was looking at her. Or maybe the real problem was she liked it too much. Yesterday she would have considered his probing gaze and bone-melting grin offensive, but this morning it made her feel all warm and mushy inside.

Kissing him had definitely been bad idea.

"I've been doing some thinking," he said, taking a few casual steps toward her.

Her heart climbed up in her throat, but she refused to let him see how nervous he was making her. "About?"

"Last night."

She was tempted to ask, *Which part?* but she had the sinking feeling she already knew. So instead she asked, in what she hoped was a bored and disinterested tone, "And?"

He continued in her direction, drawing closer with every step. "I think I've had a change of heart."

*Uh-oh.*

She hoped he meant that he'd had a change of heart

about the way he objectified the opposite sex, but somehow she didn't think so.

"Now that I know what I'll be *missing,* maybe I won't be cooperating with the family after all."

Oh, yeah, kissing him had been a *really* bad idea.

He was coming closer, that look in his eyes, like any second he planned to ravish her. And the part that really stunk was that she wanted him to. Desperately. She had assumed that playing the role of the aggressor last night, socking it to him when he was all confused and vulnerable—and a little bit adorable—would somehow put her in a position of control.

Boy, had she been wrong.

He'd managed to turn the tables on her. At that moment, she'd never felt more *out* of control in her life. And the really frightening thing was, she kind of liked it.

"I mean, what's the worst that will happen?" he said.

Hopefully something really bad. "Hanging?"

He was standing so close now that he could reach out and touch her. And though every instinct she possessed was screaming for her to back away, she wouldn't give him the satisfaction of so much as a flinch.

"And then I got to thinking." He leaned in, his face so close to hers she could smell the toothpaste on his breath. "Who says they even have to know?"

Bloody hell, was *she* in trouble. If he decided to kiss her right now, she would have no choice but to kiss him back. And then he would know the truth. That she wasn't nearly as rigid as she'd led him to believe.

His eyes locked on hers. Deep brown irises with flecks of black that seemed to bleed out from his pupils.

Full of something wicked and dangerous. And exciting. And God knew she could have used a little excitement in her life.

No, no, no! Excitement was bad. She liked things even-paced and predictable. This was just chemical.

It took everything in her, but she managed to say, with a tone as bland as her expression, "Are you finished?"

"Finished?"

"Can we go to work now?"

The grin not slipping, he finally backed away and said, "You're tough, Victoria Houghton."

Didn't she wish that were true. Didn't she wish that her heart wasn't pounding so hard it felt as though it might beat right through her rib cage. That her limbs didn't feel heavy with arousal. That her skin would stop burning to feel his touch.

*Don't let him know.*

"Yes, I am," she lied.

A playful, taunting grin lifted the corners of his lips, and he reached past her to open the door. "But I'm tougher."

By three o'clock that afternoon Victoria managed to catch up on the backlog of calls and e-mails. No thanks to Charles, who, in a fraction of that time, proved himself to be a complete pain in the neck.

He popped into her office a minute after three, for what must have been the fifth time that day. "I heard the phone ring. Any answer to the employment ad?"

He knew damned well that she had just placed the ad with the employment agency that morning and they weren't likely to hear anything until at least tomorrow.

He parked himself behind her chair, hands propped on the back, his fingers brushing the shoulders of her jacket. The hair on her arms shivered to attention and she got that tingly feeling in the pit of her belly. But telling him to back off would only give him the satisfaction of knowing that he was getting to her.

"It was your mother," she told him, leaving off the *again* that could have followed. The woman was ruthless. The kind of mother who drove her children away with affection. It probably didn't help matters that Charles was an only child and the sole focus of her adoration.

No wonder he didn't want to settle down. He was already smothered with all the female attention he could handle.

"What are you working on?" he asked, leaning casually down to peer at her computer monitor, his face so close she could feel his breath shift the hair by her ear.

"A template for an updated, more efficient call and e-mail log."

He leaned in closer to see, his cheek nearly touching hers, and, did he smell delicious. She wanted to bury her face in the crook of his neck and take a long, deep breath. Nuzzle his skin. Maybe take a nibble.

"How does it work?" he asked.

"Work?"

"The spreadsheet."

Oh, right. "When I input the number or e-mail address, it automatically lists all the other pertinent information, so you don't have to waste any time looking it up yourself. It's color-coded by urgency."

"That's brilliant," he said.

She couldn't tell if he meant it or was just being sarcastic. "Oh, yes, I'm sure they'll award me the Pulitzer. Or maybe even the Nobel Peace Prize."

The rumble of his laugh vibrated all the way through her. "You said my mother called again. What did she want this time?"

She swiveled in her chair and stuck a pile of phone messages in his face, so he had no choice but to back off or get a mouthful of fuchsia paper. "To remind you about your father's birthday party. She wanted to confirm that you're spending the *entire* weekend with them."

He took the messages and sat on the edge of her desk instead, riffling through them. "What did you tell her?"

"That you would be there. *All* weekend. And you're really looking forward to it."

He shot her a curious look. "Seriously?"

She flashed him a bright and, yes, slightly wicked smile. "Seriously."

He narrowed his eyes at her. "You didn't really."

"Oh, I did."

She could have sworn that some of the color drained from his face. "That's odd, because I seem to recall telling you to tell her that I wouldn't be able to stay the whole weekend."

"Did you?" she asked innocently. "I guess I forgot."

He knew damned well that she hadn't forgotten anything.

"That's evil," he said.

She just smiled. That was what he got for messing with her—although, in all fairness, she had been the one to kiss him. But she had the feeling that there would be nothing fair about this unspoken competition they had gotten themselves into.

"Just for that, I should drag you along with me," he told her.

A duke bringing his personal assistant home for a weekend visit with the folks. Like that would ever happen. She had the sneaking suspicion that being royals, they clung to slightly higher standards. Or maybe they would make her stay in the staff quarters and take her meals in the kitchen.

Was that what she had been reduced to? Servant's status?

She and her father may not have been megarich, but they had lived a very comfortable lifestyle. The outer edges of upper crust. And to what end? Had he only been honest, lived within their means, she wouldn't be in this mess.

But now was not the time or the place to rehash her father's betrayal.

"I could ring her and tell her you don't want to stay," she told Charles. "That you have better things to do than spend time with your parents. Although, you know, they're not getting any younger."

"Wow," he said, shaking his head. "You and my mother would get along great."

She doubted that. His mother didn't strike her as the type to socialize with the hired help.

"Was there anything else you needed?" she asked, wanting him off her desk. He was too close, smelled too good. "I'd like to get back to work."

"Pressing business?" he asked.

"Keeping up on all the calls and e-mails from your female admirers is a full-time job."

"Maybe, but right now," he said, locking his chocolate eyes on hers and leaning closer, so she was crowded against the back of her chair. "I only have one special woman in my life."

Uh-oh.

*Please, please,* Victoria silently pleaded, *let it be anyone but me.*

He held up the message slips. "And I'd better go call her and tell her just how much I'm looking forward to the party."

She let out a quiet, relieved breath.

He rose from the corner of her desk, but his scent lingered as he walked to the door. "Buzz me if you hear about the ad."

"The second I hear anything," she promised. Hoping this would be the last time she saw him until it was time to leave for the evening.

Even that would be too soon. Maybe she could just sneak out unnoticed.

It was a dangerous game they had begun playing, but she wasn't about to surrender. She wouldn't let him win. He needed to be knocked down a peg or two. Put in his place. And she was just the woman to do it.

# Eight

Charles's mother rang back not fifteen minutes later. The woman was ruthless.

Victoria struggled to sound anything but exasperated by her repeated calls. "I'm afraid he's in a meeting," she said, just as he had instructed her. In a meeting, on another line. He never took personal calls at work. "But I would be happy to take a message."

"I don't mean to bother," she said, which is how she began all of her phone conversations, whether it was the first or tenth call of the day. "I'm just calling about the party, to extend a formal invitation."

Again? Hadn't Victoria already sent an RSVP for him? How many times did she have to invite her own son? "I'll let Charles know," she said automatically.

"Oh, no, not for Charles," she said. "For *you*."

For *her?* But…

Oh, no, he didn't. He *wouldn't.* "For *me,* ma'am?"

"He told us you'll be joining him for the weekend," she gushed excitedly. And the weird thing was, she actually sounded *happy.* "I just wanted you to know how eager we are to meet you. Charles rarely brings his lady friends home."

*Lady friends?* Did she think…? "Ma'am, I *work* for Charles."

"Oh, I know. But he values your friendship. And any friend of Charles is a friend of ours. His father and I just wanted you to know that you're welcome."

Friendship? Since when were she and Charles friends?

"So, we'll see you then?" his mother asked.

Did Victoria really have the heart to tell her the truth? She sounded so genuinely eager to meet her. How could she tell her it was nothing more than a cruel trick?

So she said the only thing she could. "Yes, of course. I'll see you then."

Victoria was out of her chair before she hung up the phone. Not bothering to knock, she barged into Charles's office. And got the distinct feeling he'd been waiting for her to do just that. He was sitting back in his chair, elbows on the armrests, hands folded across his chest. But it was too late to turn around now.

"You call *me* evil?" she said.

He smiled. "I take it my mother phoned you."

"That was low, even for you."

He looked pleased with himself. "An eye for an eye. Isn't that what they say?"

"I do not what to spend a weekend at your parents's estate."

"Neither do I. But I guess neither of us has a choice now."

"They're not *my* parents. I have no obligation to be there."

He shrugged. "So, ring her back and tell her you don't want to come. I'm sure they won't be too offended."

She glared at him.

"Or, you could come with me and you might actually have fun."

"I seriously doubt that."

"Why?"

"Why? *You* don't even want to go!"

"My parents are good people. They mean well. But when it's just the three of us it can get…stifling. I get there Friday night, and by Saturday afternoon we've run out of things to talk about. With you there it might take a little bit of the pressure off."

"I wouldn't have a clue what to say to your parents. They're completely out of my league."

His brow edged into a frown. "How do you figure?"

"I'm an *employee* of the royal family."

"So what? You're still a person. We're all just people."

Was he really so naive? Did he truly not understand the way the world worked? They were royalty, and she was, and always would be, a nobody in their eyes. Or was this just part of the game he was playing? Lure her to his parent's estate so he could humiliate her in front of his entire family?

His intentions weren't even the issue. The real problem was that she simply didn't trust him.

"You know, you don't give yourself nearly enough credit." He rose from his chair and she tensed, thinking he might come toward her, but he walked around to sit on the edge of his desk instead. Since he'd last been in her office he'd taken off his jacket, loosened his tie, and rolled the sleeves of his dress shirt to his elbows. He seemed to do that every day, after his last meeting.

Casual as he looked, though, he still radiated an air of authority. He was always in control.

Well, almost always.

"Tell me," he said. "How could a woman so accomplished have such a low self-esteem?"

"It has nothing to do with self-esteem. Which I have my fair share of, thank you very much. It's just the way the world works."

"When you met my cousins, did they look down their noses at you?"

"Of course not."

"I think my parents might surprise you. It can't hurt to come with me and find out. Besides, the party should be a blast. Good food and company. And if at any time you feel uncomfortable, I'll take you home."

If she went at all, she would be driving herself. *If* she went?

She couldn't believe she was actually contemplating this. If nothing else, out of curiosity. At least, that's what she preferred to tell herself. There were other possible motivations that were far too disturbing to consider. Like wanting to see the kind of man Charles was around his family. What he was *really* like.

"Fine. I'll go." she said. Then added, "It's not as though I have much choice."

"Smashing," he said, looking truly pleased, which had her seriously doubting her decision.

What was he up to?

"We leave in the afternoon, two weeks from this Friday and return Sunday afternoon."

"I'll meet you there," she said. She wanted her car, in case she needed a quick getaway. And surprisingly, he didn't argue.

"Pack casual," he said. "But the party Saturday night is formal."

Formal? She was expecting an intimate family gathering. Not a social event. "How many people will be there?"

He shrugged. "No more than a hundred or so."

One *hundred?* Her heart seized in her chest. All more wealthy and influential than her.

Smashing.

"You have a dress?" he asked.

From a charity event four years ago. It would be completely out of fashion by now. She didn't exactly have the money to spend on expensive gowns. And for a party like this, nothing less than the best would do.

"I'm sure I can scrounge something up," she said, hoping she sounded more confident than she was feeling.

"You're sure?" he asked. "If it's a strain on the budget right now—"

"It's fine," she snapped. That was the second time

he'd made a reference to her diminishing funds. "It isn't as though I'm destitute."

He held his hands up defensively. "Relax. I wasn't suggesting that."

*My God, listen to yourself.* Maybe Charles was right. Maybe her self-esteem had taken a hit lately. Maybe her confidence was shot. Why else would she be so touchy?

Maybe she needed to get out with people. Reestablish her sense of self. Or something like that.

She softened her tone. "I'm sorry. I didn't mean to snap."

"If you really don't want to go to the party—"

"I'll go," she said firmly. "For the whole weekend."

Who knows, maybe a short vacation would be good for her. A chance to forget about the shambles her life was currently in and just relax.

And who knew? She might even have fun.


Victoria unlocked her flat door at exactly seven-thirty the following evening. Early by her standards, yet it had felt like the longest day of her life.

Since she'd kissed Charles the other night, then accepted his offer to join him at his parents, the teasing and sexual innuendo hadn't ceased. When they were alone, anyway. When anyone else was around he was nothing but professional. He treated her more like a peer than a subordinate. It was his way of showing that he did indeed respect her.

And maybe the teasing wasn't as bad as it had been at first. Not so immoral. Not that she would allow it to progress to anything more than that.

She dropped her purse and keys on the hall table and headed straight for the wine rack, draping her suit jacket on the back of the couch along the way. She opened a bottle of cabernet, her favorite wine, poured herself a generous glass, kicked off her pumps, and collapsed on the couch.

Charles left work at the same time, making sure to let her know, in the elevator on the way down to the parking structure, that he had a dinner date. As if she cared one way or the other how or with whom he chose to spend his free time. Although she couldn't help wondering who the unlucky girl could be. Amber from the club, perhaps? Or maybe Zoey from the fund-raiser last Friday? Or a dozen others who had called him in the past few days. Or maybe someone new.

Whoever she was, Victoria was just glad it wasn't her.

*Are you really?* an impish little voice in her head asked. *Aren't you even a little curious to know what the big deal is? Why so many women fall at his feet? They can't all be after his money and title.*

It had to be the wine. It was going straight to her head. Probably because she'd skipped lunch. Again.

*You'll waste away to nothing,* her father used to warn her, in regard to her spotty eating habits. And it would certainly explain her peculiar lack of energy. Not to mention the noisy rumble in her stomach. She sipped her wine and made a mental list of what was in her refrigerator.

Leftover Thai from three days ago that was probably spoiled by now. A few cups of fat-free yogurt, sour skim milk and a slightly shriveled, partial head of romaine lettuce. The contents of the freezer weren't much more promising. A few frozen dinners long past their expiration date and a bag of desiccated, ice-encrusted peas.

She was weeks past due for a trip to the market, but lately there never seemed to be time. Besides, she'd never been much of a cook. There had never been time to learn. On late nights at the Houghton she ate dinner in her office, or their housekeeper doubled as a cook when the need arose. In fact, in her entire life Victoria had never cooked an entire meal by herself. She wasn't even sure if she knew how.

Nor did she have the inclination to learn.

She sat up and grabbed the pile of carryout menus on the coffee table. The sushi place around the corner was right on top.

That would work.

She grabbed the cordless phone and was preparing to dial when the bell chimed for the door. Who could that be? She hoped it wasn't her father. She hadn't returned any of his calls, and he was probably getting impatient.

Maybe if she didn't answer, whoever it was would go away.

She waited a moment, holding her breath, then the bell chimed again.

With a groan she set the phone and her nearly empty glass on the coffee table and dragged herself up from the couch, a touch dizzy from the wine, and picked her way to the door. She peered through the peephole, surprised to find not her father but Charles standing there.

What in heaven's name did *he* want?

She considered not opening the door, but he'd probably

seen her car parked out front and knew she was home. She just couldn't force herself to be rude.

She unlatched the chain, pulled the door open and asked, "What do you want?"

Despite her sharp tone, he smiled. He was still wearing his work clothes. Well put together, but with just a hint of the end-of-the-day rumples. And he looked absolutely delicious.

*Bite your tongue, Vic.*

"I realized I still owe you dinner," he said. In his hand he held a carryout bag from the very restaurant she had just been about to phone. As though he had somehow read her mind.

That was just too weird.

"I hope you like sushi," he said, shouldering his way past her into her flat. Uninvited yet again.

So why wasn't she doing anything to stop him?

"And if I don't like sushi?" she asked, following him to the kitchen.

"Then you wouldn't have a menu for a sushi restaurant conveniently by the phone." He set the bag on the counter. "Would you?"

How did he…?

He must have seen it there that morning. The first time he barged in uninvited. "I thought you had a date."

The idea that someone stood him up was satisfying somehow, although, what it really meant was she was his second choice. The veritable booby prize.

"I do." He set the bag on the countertop and grinned. "With you."

What was it she just felt? Relieved? Flattered?

Highly doubtful.

She folded her arms across her chest. "I don't think it can be considered a date when the other party knows nothing about it."

He pasted an innocent look on his face. "Did I forget to tell you?"

He took off his jacket and handed it to her. Like an idiot, she took it. And came this close to lifting it to her nose to breathe in his scent, rubbing her cheek against the fabric. She caught herself at the last second and folded it over her arm instead.

*Stop it, Vic.*

He wasn't paying attention, anyway. He was busy emptying the bag, opening the carryout containers.

The aroma of the sushi wafted her way, making her mouth water. And if she didn't eat something soon, the wine was going to give her a doozy of a headache.

"I'll have dinner with you," she said, then added, "just this once."

He shrugged, as though her refusing his company had never even crossed his mind. Could he be more arrogant? Or more cute?

No, no, no! He is not cute.

It took only a few disastrous office romances to make her vow never to get involved with a coworker again. Not to mention the other laundry list of reasons she would never get involved with a man like him.

This was just dinner.

"I wasn't sure what you liked, so I got a variety," he said.

"I guess." There was enough there to feed half a dozen people. She would have some left over for lunch and dinner tomorrow. And since he went through all this trouble, the least she could do is offer him a drink. "I just opened a bottle of cabernet."

"I thought you would never ask," he said with a grin, then gestured to the cupboards. "You have plates?"

"To the left of the sink." She draped his jacket neatly over the back of the couch over her own and poured him a glass of wine, then refilled her own glass. She really should slow down, wait to drink until she'd eaten something, but the warm glow of inebriation felt good just then. And it wasn't as if she was completely sloshed or anything. Just pleasantly buzzed.

The dining table was topped with half-unpacked boxes, so she carried their glasses to the coffee table instead. It was that or eat standing up in the kitchen, and she honestly didn't think her legs would hold her up for long. She considered going back into the kitchen to help him, but the couch looked so inviting, she flopped down and made herself comfortable. Some hostess she was, making him serve her dinner. But he didn't seem to mind.

Besides, that's what he got for showing up out of the blue.

"Do you have a serving platter?" Charles called from the kitchen.

"Somewhere in this mess," she said. The truth was she usually just ate straight from the carryout containers. "I haven't gotten that far in my unpacking." She paused, guilt getting the best of her, and called, "Do you want help?"

"No, I've got it."

Good. She rested her head back on the cushions, sipped her wine, and closed her eyes. When she opened them again, he was setting everything down on the coffee table.

"Wake up. Time to eat."

"Just resting my eyes," she said. She sat up and he sat down beside her, so close their thighs were touching. His was solid and warm. She didn't normally let her size bother her, but he just seemed so large in comparison. Intimidating, although not in a threatening way, if that made any sense at all. And, God help her, he was sexy as hell with his collar open and his sleeves rolled up.

She took a tuna roll, dipped it in soy sauce, and popped it into her mouth. He did the same. The delicious flavors were completely lost on her as she watched him eat. He even managed to chew sexy, if that was possible.

She peeled her eyes away, before he noticed her staring, just as the doorbell chimed again.

"Expecting someone?" he asked, like maybe she had a date with some other man that had slipped her mind.

"Not that I recall." She sighed irritably and dragged herself up and walked to the door.

If she weren't so relaxed from the wine, she would have remembered to check the peephole. And if she had, she would have seen it was her father standing there.

# Nine

Victoria stepped into the hall and edged the door shut behind her so her father wouldn't see who was sitting on her couch. "Daddy, what are you doing here?"

"You haven't returned my calls. I was concerned."

I'll bet you were, she thought. *Concerned that all of those lies have started catching up to you.* The idea made her heart hurt, but she was too angry to cut him any slack right now.

Besides, now was not the time for that unpleasant discussion. "I'm a little busy right now."

"Too busy for your own father?" He looked old and tired, but she couldn't feel sympathy for him.

She needed another day to think about exactly what she wanted to say to him. Not that she'd thought of much else lately. Maybe she just needed time to be less angry. "I'll call you tomorrow."

His mouth fell open and he stared at her, aghast, as though he couldn't believe she would deny him entrance into her home. "Victoria, I demand to know what's going on."

The door pulled open and Charles appeared behind her wearing a concerned expression. "Everything okay, Victoria?"

She knew he meant well, he was being protective, and in many instances she might have appreciated his intervention.

Now was not one of them.

He'd just done more harm than good.

"What is he doing here?" her father said, spitting out the question.

As if she owed him any explanation at all. Or cared that he was displeased. "Having dinner."

"Dinner?" he said, not bothering to hide his disdain. "You're having dinner with *him?*"

"Yes, I am."

He looked from her to Charles, and she knew exactly what he was thinking. "Are you—?"

"It's just dinner," she said, not that it was any of his business. "And right now you should leave. We'll talk about this another time."

But her father wasn't listening. He was too angry. He knew better than to let himself get upset. It wasn't good for his heart. Or maybe his heart was just fine now, and that was a lie, too.

"How could you do this to me?" he asked. "How could you betray me this way?"

How could *she* do this? Who was he to accuse her of deception? "There's been some betrayal going on, but it certainly isn't coming from my end."

"What do you mean?" He shot Charles a venomous glare. "What has he been telling you?"

"What you should have told me a long time ago."

The angry facade slipped a fraction. "I don't know what you're talking about."

"I saw the files from the sale of the hotel, Daddy. I know about all of your debt. All the lies you told me."

"He's trying to turn you against me."

He was still going to deny it? Lie to her face? At the very least she had expected a humbled apology, maybe a plea for forgiveness. Instead he continued to try to deceive her?

She wanted to grab him and shake some sense into him. She was stunned and angry and hurt. And even worse, she was disappointed. All of her life she had looked up to him. Idolized him even. But he had changed that forever.

"The only one doing that is you, Daddy," she said sadly, knowing that she would never look at her father the same way again.

"I should go," Charles said, taking a step backward from the door. This was a little too intense for his taste. Had he known it was her father at the door, he never would have interfered. He had enough of his own family issues to deal with without taking on someone else's.

Victoria held up a hand to stop him. "No. You stay. *You* were invited. My father is the one who needs to go."

Technically, Charles had shown up unannounced and muscled his way inside. But he didn't think now was the time to argue with her.

"I can't believe you're choosing him over me," her father said.

"And I can't believe you're still lying to me," she shot back, although she sounded more resigned than angry. "Until you can be honest with me, we have nothing left to say to each other."

Before her father could utter another word, she shut the door and flipped the deadbolt, and for several seconds she just stood there. Maybe waiting for him to have a change of heart.

After a moment of silence, she rose up on her toes and peered out the peephole. She sighed quietly, then turned to face Charles and leaned against the door. "He's gone."

"Victoria, I'm really sorry. I didn't mean to—"

"It's not your fault. He's the one who lied to me. He's *still* lying to me."

"I'm sure he'll come around."

She shook her head. "I'm not so sure. You have no idea how stubborn he can be."

If he was anything like Victoria, Charles had a pretty good idea. "What are you going to do?"

"I'm not sure. But I do know what I'm not going to do."

"What's that?"

"All my life I've been doing what my father asked of me. What was *expected* of me. Not anymore."

She surprised him by taking his hand, lacing her fingers through his. She gave it a tug. "Come on."

"Where?"

"Where do you think, genius? To my bedroom."

Wait…what? How had they jumped from dinner to her bedroom? "I beg your pardon?"

He'd been out to get in her knickers since the day he met her. And it certainly wouldn't be the first time he'd taken advantage of a situation to seduce a woman— although she seemed to be doing most of the seducing now. Not to mention that he had a strong suspicion she was slightly intoxicated. Again, that had never stopped him before. Yet, something about this just didn't feel right.

He actually felt…guilty.

She tugged again and he felt his feet moving.

"Hey, don't get me wrong," he said, as he let her lead him down the hall. "I'm not one to pass up revenge sex, but are you sure this is a good idea?"

"I think it's an excellent idea." She dragged him into the bedroom and switched on the lamp beside her bed. Only then did she let go of his hand.

Like the rest of the flat, there were boxes everywhere, but in the dim light the bed looked especially inviting. And oh, so tempting.

But he knew he really shouldn't.

She turned to him and started unbuttoning her blouse.

Christ, she was making it really hard to do the right thing. "Maybe we should step back a second, so you can think about what you're doing."

She gazed up at him though thick, dark lashes. "I

know exactly what I'm doing." The blouse slipped from her shoulders and fluttered silently to the carpet.

Ah, hell.

Underneath she wore a lacy black bra. Sexier than he would have imagined for her. But he'd always suspected, or maybe fantasized, there was more to Victoria. That deep down there was a temptress just waiting to break free.

It looked like he was right.

She reached behind her to unzip her skirt, and desire curled low and deep in his gut. "Are you just going to stand there?" she asked.

"I just don't want you to do something you'll regret." Where was he getting this crap? When did he ever care if a woman had regrets? Was he, God forbid, growing a conscience?

"I'm a big girl. I can handle it." She eased the skirt down her legs, hips swaying seductively, and let it fall in a puddle at her feet. She wore a matching black lace thong and thigh-high stockings. And her body? It was damn near perfect. In fact, he was pretty sure it *was* perfect. And he was so mesmerized that for a minute, he forgot to breathe.

"You've been after me for days," she said. "Don't chicken out now."

Calling him a chicken was a little harsh, considering two days ago she'd accused him of disrespect toward the opposite sex. The woman was a walking contradiction. But an extremely sexy and desirable one.

His favorite kind.

She walked toward him—stalked him was more like

it—and reached up to unfasten the buttons of his shirt. She did look as though she knew what she was doing.

One button, two buttons. He really should stop her. It wouldn't take much. Although he suspected that if he turned her down now, he wouldn't get another chance.

Damn it. It shouldn't be this complicated. Maybe that was what was really bothering him. This had complex and messy written all over it.

One more button, then another. Then she pushed his shirt off his shoulders and down his arms. She gazed up at him, sighing with satisfaction, her eyes sleepy and soft. She flattened her hands on his chest, dragging her nails lightly across his skin all the way to his waistband. She toyed with the clasp on his slacks...

Oh, what the hell.

He circled an arm around her waist and dragged her against him. Her surprised gasp was the last thing he heard before he crushed his mouth down on hers. Hard.

She groaned and looped her arms around his neck, fingers sinking through his hair. Feeding off his mouth.

He scooped her up off her feet and they tumbled onto the mattress together. She was so small he worried he might crush her, but she managed to wriggle out from under him, push him onto his back so she could get at the zipper of his slacks. Then she shoved them, along with his boxers, down his hips, and he kicked them away.

"My goodness," she said, gazing down at him with a marginally stunned expression. "We've certainly been blessed, haven't we?"

Though he hadn't considered it until just then, she was awfully petite. What if she was that small everywhere?

"Too much for you?" he asked.

"Let's hope not." She took a deep breath and blew it out. "Condom?"

"In my wallet, in my jacket." Which was in the other room.

"Right back," she said, hopping up from the bed and darting from the room. A bundle of sexual energy. She was back in seconds, long before he had time to talk any sense into himself.

Who was he kidding? They were already well past the point of no return. Besides, she didn't appear to be having any second thoughts.

He sat up and she tossed him his wallet. He fished a condom out, then, realizing one probably wasn't going to cut it—he hoped—he grabbed one more.

"You're sure those will fit?" she asked, but he could see that she was teasing.

"They're extra large," he assured her, setting his wallet and both condoms on the bedside table.

Victoria stood beside the bed, gazing at him with hungry eyes. She unhooked the front clasp on her bra and peeled it off, revealing breasts that couldn't have been more amazing. Not very big, but in perfect proportion to the rest of her. High and firm. The perfect mouthful. And he couldn't wait to get a taste.

She walked to the bed, easing her thong down and kicking it into the pile with the rest of her clothes. He decided, now that he'd seen the whole package, she really was perfect.

And just for tonight, she was all his.

Though he usually liked to be the one in charge, he

didn't protest when she pushed him down onto his back and climbed on him, straddling his thighs, her stockings soft and slippery against his skin. What he really wanted was to feel them wrapped around his shoulders, but she had something entirely different in mind. She grabbed one of the condoms and had it out of the package and rolled into place in the span of one raspy breath.

It was a surreal feeling, lying there beneath her, and the fact that *she* had seduced him and not the other way around. She was unlike any woman he had been with before. Most tried too hard to impress him, to be what they thought he wanted. For Victoria, it just seemed to come naturally. She leaned down and kissed him, teasing at first. Just a brush of her lips, and a brief sweep of her tongue. She tasted like wine and desire. And when she touched him, raked her nails lightly down his chest, he shivered. She seemed to know instinctively what to do to drive him nuts.

They kissed and touched, teased each other until he did not think he could take much more. Victoria must have been thinking the same thing.

She locked her eyes on his, lowered herself over him and took him inside her. Tentatively at first. She was so slick and hot, so small and tight, he almost lost it on that first slow, downward slide. Then she stopped, and for an instant he was afraid he really might be too much for her, too big. But her expression said he was anything but. It said that she could handle anything he could dish out, and then some. It said that she wanted this just as much as he did.

She rose up, slowly, until only the very tip remained

inside of her. She hovered there for several seconds, torturing him, then, with her eyes still trained on his, sank back down, her body closing like a fist around him. He groaned, teetering on the edge of an explosion. In his life he'd never seen or felt anything more erotic. And if she did that one more time, he *was* going to lose it.

He rolled her over onto her back and plunged into her. She arched up against him, gasping, her eyes widening with shock because he was so deep.

He nearly stopped, to ask her if she was okay, but she was clawing at his back, hooking her legs around his hips, urging him closer, and that said everything he needed to know. He may have been bigger than her, but they fit together just fine. He stopped worrying about hurting her. All he could think about was the way it felt. The way *she* felt. And every thrust brought him that much closer to the edge.

The last coherent thought he had was that this was too good, too perfect, then Victoria shuddered and cried out, her body tensing around him, and he couldn't think at all as she coaxed him into oblivion with her.

# Ten

Victoria lay in bed beside Charles, watching him sleep. Typical man. Have sex three or four times then go out like a light.

He looked so peaceful. So…satisfied. A feeling she definitely shared.

In her experience, first times always tended to be a little awkward or uncomfortable. But there was nothing awkward about the way Charles had touched her. She'd once believed that just because a man looked like he would be good in the sack didn't necessarily mean he would be, but Charles had completely blown that theory to smithereens as well.

In fact, he was so ridiculously wonderful, so skilled with his hands and his mouth and every other part of his body, it should have given her pause. He'd obviously had a lot of practice. Yet when he looked at her and touched her, it was as though there had never been anyone else.

It was almost enough to make her go mushy-brained. And she probably would have if she weren't so firmly rooted in reality.

At least now she knew what all the fuss was about.

For a minute there, when he'd first taken off his pants, she honestly thought the size difference might be an issue, but in the end the tight fit and the wonderful friction it created had been the best part. Remarkable size wasn't worth much if a man didn't know how to use it.

And, oh, he did.

The second best part was the knowledge that she was doing something totally wrong for her. Wrong on so many levels. She'd always been the obedient daughter, doing as she was told. She never imagined that a simple thing like being bad could feel *so* good.

But it's just sex, she reminded herself, lest she get carried away and start having actual feelings for him.

She was sure that things would be clearer in the morning, at which point she would realize what she'd really done and feel overwhelming regret. Especially when she got to the office. Wouldn't *that* be awkward? But until then she was going to enjoy it.

She curled up against him under the covers, soaking up his warmth. He sighed in his sleep and wrapped an arm around her.

Nice. Very nice.

She closed her eyes, felt herself drifting off. When she

opened her eyes again, the morning sunlight was peeking through the blinds, and Charles was already gone.

Sleeping with Charles had been a *really* bad idea.

Victoria stood in the elevator at work as it climbed, dreading the moment it reached her floor. The hollow *ting* as the doors slid open plucked every one of her frayed nerves.

He hadn't even had the decency to wake her before he left. He'd just skulked away in the middle of the night. Probably the way he did with all the women he slept with.

*Did you really think you were any different?*

She had gone from feeling sexy and desirable, feeling *bad,* to feeling…cheap.

He could have at least said goodbye before he left. Maybe given her one last kiss.

You are not going to let this bother you, she told herself as she exited the elevator and walked to her office. Penelope, who typically ignored her, lifted her head as she passed and actually looked at her. Not a nasty look. Just sort of…blank.

*She knows. She knows what Charles and I did.*

That was ridiculous. It was just a coincidence that she chose today to acknowledge Victoria. After all, she doubted Charles confided in his secretary about his sex life. And how else would she possibly know?

So this was what it felt like to be the office slut.

Fantastic.

Victoria nodded at the old prune, then opened her office door. Feeling edgy and unsettled, she hung her jacket, sat in her chair, and stowed her purse in the bottom desk drawer. Work as usual. This day was no different than any other. Not to mention, this situation was temporary. With any luck, she would hear from the employment agency about a suitable replacement.

She was just about boot to up her computer when the intercom buzzed, startling her half to death, and Charles's voice, in a very professional tone, said, "Would you please come in here, Victoria?"

Her heart jumped up into her throat.

Here we go, the part where he tells you it was fun but it isn't going to happen again. He certainly wasn't wasting any time. Not that she hadn't expected that.

She pressed the call button. "One minute."

The sooner it's over the better. And only once, for a millisecond, would she allow herself to admit that she was the tiniest bit disappointed it had to end. It may have only been sex, but it was damned good sex.

She remembered the invitation to spend the weekend with his family and cringed. That would just be too awkward. She would have to come up with some reason to decline. She doubted he would be anything but relieved.

What had she been thinking? One night of fantastic sex was not worth all of this complication.

She took a deep breath. No point in putting this off any longer. She rose from her chair, walked to the door and pulled it open, stepping inside his office. But he wasn't sitting at his desk.

The door closed behind her, and the next thing she knew, she was in Charles's arms.

"Morning," he said, a wicked grin on his face, and

before she could utter a sound, he was kissing her. Deep and sweet and wonderful. And though everything in her was screaming that this was wrong, she wrapped her arms around his neck and kissed him back.

She didn't care that he was kissing away her lipstick, or rumpling her hair. She just wanted to feel him. To be close to him.

Oh, this was bad.

When he broke the kiss she felt dizzy and breathless. He grinned down at her and said, "Good morning."

She couldn't resist returning the smile. Despite feeling as though her entire world had been flopped upside down, she actually felt…happy.

"If it weren't for the conference call I had this morning," he said, caressing her cheek with the tips of his fingers, "we might still be in bed."

"Conference call?" He left because he had to be at work?

"At six-thirty. You didn't get my note?"

"Note?" He left a note?

"On the pillow."

The rush of pure relief made her weak in the knees. And she didn't even care how wrong it was. "I guess I didn't see it."

A grin curled his mouth. "You didn't think I'd just up and leave without a word, did you?"

She shrugged, feeling ashamed of herself for thinking that. For judging him that way. And automatically assuming the worst. "It doesn't matter."

"Have time to take a break?" he asked with a devilish smile.

"I just got here."

He dipped his head to nibble on her neck. "I don't think your boss will mind."

Office romance. Very bad idea. But neither the affair nor the job were going to last long, so, honestly, why the hell not? Besides, it was really tough to think logically when his hands were sneaking under her clothing, searching for bare skin.

"What about Penelope?" she asked.

He shuddered and shook his head. "Definitely not my type."

She laughed. "That's not what I meant."

"I already told her that I'm not to be disturbed." He kissed her throat, her chin, nibbled the corner of her lips. "It's just you and me."

The old woman would have to be a fool not to realize what was going on, but she already disliked Victoria, so what difference did it make? Besides, Victoria had never been one to care what other people thought of her.

"I'm sure I can spare a minute or two," she said.

He smiled. "It's going to be a lot longer than a minute or two."

He lifted her up in his arms and carried her to the couch. He seemed to like doing that. Taking over, seizing control. And for some reason she didn't mind. Probably because he made her feel so damned good. He was one of those rare lovers who took pleasure for himself only after she had been satisfied first. She had always heard that men like that existed, but she'd never actually met one.

He sat on the couch and set her in his lap. But before he could kiss her, she asked, "Have you done this before?"

"What do you mean?"

"In here, with another assistant." She didn't know where the question came from, or if she even wanted to know the answer. And he looked surprised that she'd asked.

"You know what, never mind. Forget I asked."

She tried to kiss him, before she completely killed the mood, but he caught her face in his hands.

"Hold on, I want to answer that." His eyes locked on hers and he said, "No, Victoria, I haven't."

The way he said it, the way he looked her in the eye, made her believe it was the truth. She had no reason, no *right* to be relieved, but she was. And the tiny part of her that was still doubtful melted into a puddle at their feet.

She wanted this, right here, right now, and she wasn't going to be afraid to take it.


It was almost noon when Victoria finally made it back to her office. And she'd barely been there fifteen minutes, checking phone messages—there were already three from his mother—when Charles quietly opened the door and slipped inside.

She pretended not to hear him skulking around behind her, but when she felt his hands on her shoulders, his lips teasing the back of her neck, he became really hard to ignore.

"Neither of us is going to get anything done if you keep this up," she scolded, but she wasn't doing any-thing to stop him. Although, she thought, maybe she should. Unlike his office, hers didn't have a sturdy lock. In fact, she wasn't sure if it locked at all.

"Just thought I would pop in and say hello," he said, his breath warm on her skin. She couldn't deny that another hour or so in his office was tempting.

No, you have work to do.

"Your smother called," she said. "Several times."

He stopped kissing her. "My what?"

She turned to look at him. He had a quirky grin on his face. "Your mother," she repeated.

"That's not what you said."

What was he talking about? "Yes I did."

He shook his head. "No. You said *smother*. 'My smother called.'"

She slapped a hand over her mouth. Oh my gosh, had she? Had she really said it out loud? "I'm so sorry. That was completely inappropriate."

Rather than look offended, he laughed. "No. That's perfect. 'My smother.' I'll have to tell my father that one."

"No!" What would his father think of Victoria? Insulting his wife like that.

Charles just shrugged. "He knows what she's like. She drives everyone crazy. He'll think it's hilarious."

She swiveled in her chair to face him. "Please don't, Charles. It's going to be awkward enough. I would be mortified."

He didn't look like he got it, but he nodded. "All right. I won't say anything."

"Thank you."

He backed away from her. She couldn't help wondering if she'd offended him somehow, and she realized the idea truly disturbed her. How quickly she'd gone from disliking him to valuing his friendship.

Too fast.

And when he smiled at her, she realized he wasn't the least bit offended. "Can I take you out to dinner tonight?" he asked.

Two nights in a row? Then again, sitting in bed naked feeding each other sushi couldn't really be counted as having dinner out. And her first impulse was to say yes, she would love to. But did she want to make a habit of being seen with him in public? To be crowned his latest conquest? Just another fling? Even though that was exactly what she was.

"I don't think that would be a good idea," she said.

"Why?"

"We're sleeping together, not dating."

He shrugged. "What's the difference?"

"There's a *huge* difference. Sex is temporary. Superficial."

"And dating isn't? According to whom?"

He had a point. "I suppose it can be, but…it's just *different*."

"I don't date women with the intention of a lasting relationship. So by definition, dating for me is very temporary." He paused, then his brow tucked with concern. "You're not looking for a relationship, are you?"

"With *you?* Of course not!"

He looked relieved, and she knew enough not to take it personally. He was just establishing parameters. It was what men like him did. And it was the truth. He was the last man on earth that she would ever consider for a serious relationship.

"Well, then, what's the problem?" he asked.

"Maybe another time."

He folded his arms over his chest. "You're going to make me chase you, is that it?"

"Chase me? Are you forgetting that I was the one who had to drag you to my bedroom last night?"

"Oh yeah." That devilish, sexy grin was back, and it warmed her from the inside out. He leaned in closer, resting his hands on the arms of her chair. She couldn't help but think, *Oh, boy, here we go again.* "Did I forget to tell you how much I enjoyed it?"

He'd told her several times, but what she'd found even more endearing, most appealing, was that he had been worried about her state of mind, that she might have been acting rashly and making a mistake. She hadn't expected that from a man like him.

Every time she thought she had him pegged, he surprised her.

"Don't you have work to do?" she asked.

He dipped in close and kissed her neck, just below her ear. He'd discovered last night that it was the second most sensitive spot on her body. And he used it to his advantage. "Have dinner with me, Victoria."

She closed her eyes and her head just sort of fell back on its own. "I can't."

"It doesn't have to be a restaurant." He nibbled her earlobe and she shivered. "I'll make us dinner at my place."

Dinner at his house wouldn't be so bad. *But two nights in a row? Won't that be pushing it a little?* Although what he was doing felt awfully good. Could she honestly work up the will to deny herself another night of unconditional pleasure? "I shouldn't," she said, but not with much conviction.

"I'm an excellent cook," he coaxed, pulling her blouse aside to nibble on her shoulder. "My specialty is dessert."

He kissed his way down to her cleavage and a whimper of pleasure purled in her throat. "Well, I do have dry cleaning to drop off. I suppose I could hang around for a little while. And if you happen to have dinner ready…"

He eased himself down on the floor in front of her chair, then pulled her blouse aside, exposing one lace cup of her bra. He took her in his mouth, lace and all, and bit down lightly. Though she tried to hold it in, a moan slipped from her lips.

God, he was good.

He looked up at her with that devilish gleam. "So you'll be stopping by when? Around seven?"

"Seven sounds about right," she said, aware that her door wasn't locked and anyone could walk in. Not that anyone but him ever did. But it was the sense of danger, the possibility that someone *could,* that made her so bloody hot for him. "We really shouldn't do this in here."

"Do what?" He switched to the opposite side and took that one into his mouth.

She grabbed his head, sinking her nails though his hair. "Have sex."

"Who says we're going to have sex?"

"I guess I just assumed."

"Nah." He eased her skirt up around her hips, hooked

his fingers on her thong and dragged it down her legs. He nipped at the flesh on the inside of her upper thigh, the number-one most sensitive area on her body, and she melted into a puddle in her chair.

"Well, then, what would you call it?" she asked, her voice thick with arousal.

He grinned up at her. "Afternoon snack?"

Well, whatever he called it, as he kissed his way upward, she had the sneaking suspicion that neither of them was going to get much work done today.

# Eleven

Victoria woke slowly the next morning aware, even before she opened her eyes, something was different. Then it dawned on her.

She wasn't at home.

She was curled up in Charles's bed, warm and cozy between his soft silk sheets.

*Too* warm and cozy.

She hadn't meant to fall asleep here and risk having someone see her car parked out front. Not to mention that spending the night was just a bad idea. She had planned to go back to her own place, sleep in her own bed. Charles hadn't made it easy, though.

Last night, every time she'd made noises like she was going to leave, he would start kissing her and touching her, and she would forget what she'd been saying. And *thinking*. And when they weren't devouring each other, they lay side by side and talked. About her childhood and his. Which couldn't have been more different.

After a while it got so late, and she'd felt so sleepy. She remembered thinking that she would close her eyes for just five or ten minutes, then she would crawl back into her clothes and drive home.

So much for that plan.

He knew it, too. Charles knew she wanted to leave, and he let her sleep anyway. She wasn't sure how to take that. Most men considered letting a woman spend the night in their house too personal. Did he genuinely want her there, or was it some sort of power play? To see if he could bend her to his will. Did he do that with all of the women he *dated?*

Speaking of Charles…

She reached over and patted the mattress beside her, but encountered only cool, slippery silk.

He had one of those enormous king-size deals that a person could lie spread-eagled in and still not encounter the person lying beside them.

She reached even farther, with the very tips of her fingers, till she hit the opposite edge of the bed.

No one there.

She rose up on her elbow, pried one eye open and peered around. The curtains were drawn and Charles was nowhere to be seen.

*Here we go again,* she thought. Waking up alone. But how far could he have run this time, seeing as how they were in his house?

Not that he had *run* yesterday morning. He'd gone to work. And he'd left a note.

She sat up and rubbed her eyes. A robe hung over the side of the bed that she was guessing he'd put there for her to use. Thoughtful, yet she couldn't help wondering if all of the women who slept over wore it. Would it smell of someone else's perfume? Would she find strands of another woman's hair caught in the collar? Or did he have the decency to wash it between uses?

His shirt from the night before was draped over the chair across the room, so she padded across the cold wood floor and slipped that on instead. It hung to her knees, and she had to roll the sleeves about ten times, but it was soft and it smelled like him. And she could say with certainty that no other woman had worn it recently.

She stopped in the bathroom and saw that she had a serious case of bed head. An inconvenience of short hair. She rubbed it briskly and picked it into shape as best she could. Next to the sink was a toothbrush still in the package. For her, she assumed.

The man thought of everything. Convenient, if not a little disturbing. He probably had a whole closet full of them. For every woman he brought home.

She brushed her teeth and considered showering, but the stall was dry, and she recalled him saying something about the granite just being sealed the other day. She ventured out into the hallway instead, wondering where he could be.

She poked her head in a few of the rooms, called, "Hello!" But he didn't seem to be anywhere upstairs. Then she caught the scent of freshly brewed coffee wafting up from the lower level, and let her nose lead her to the source.

She found Charles in the kitchen, standing by the sink, the financial section of the newspaper in one hand, a cup of coffee in the other. He was dressed in a pair of threadbare jeans and nothing else, and his hair was even a little rumpled. Very *normal* looking. He looked up and smiled when she stepped in the room. "Good morning."

"Morning."

He eyed her up and down appreciatively. "I left a robe out for you, but honestly, I think I prefer the shirt." He put down the paper and cup, and walked toward her, a hungry, devilish look in his eye, and her stomach did a backflip with a triple twist.

They'd slept together on two separate occasions, so shouldn't that intense little thrill have disappeared by now? Before she could form another thought he wrapped her up in his arms and kissed her senseless, which made her thankful she'd taken the time to brush her teeth.

It should have been awkward or uncomfortable, but it wasn't. It was as though she had spent the night dozens of times before. Maybe he'd had so many women sleep over that it had become second nature waking with a virtual stranger in his house.

Okay, she wasn't a stranger, but still…

She sighed and rested her head on his chest. This was nice. It was…comfortable. Still, she couldn't shake the feeling she was just one insignificant piece to a much larger puzzle that was Charles's romantic life.

"You do this often?" she asked.

"Do what?"

"Sleepovers."

"I'm assuming you mean with women." He eased back to look at her. "Why do you ask?"

She shrugged. "You just seem to have a routine."

His brow perked with curiosity. "I do?"

"The robe, the toothbrush. It was just very…convenient."

"And here I thought I was being polite." He didn't look offended exactly. Maybe a little hurt.

She realized she was being ridiculous. Besides, she didn't want him to get the wrong idea, to think she was being possessive. Because she wasn't.

"I'm sorry," she said. "Forget I said anything. I'm obviously not very good at this."

He grinned down at her. "Oh, no, you were very good. And to answer your question about sleepovers— If I like a woman, and want to spend time with her, I invite her to stay over. Simple as that."

And why shouldn't he? Who was she to judge him? Who he did or didn't spend the night with was none of her business, anyway. She did appreciate his honesty, though.

"Now that we have that out of the way," he said. "Can I interest you in a nonroutine cup of coffee?"

She smiled up at him. "I'd love one."

"Cream or sugar?"

"A little of both."

He grabbed the cup that was already sitting beside his state-of-the-art coffeemaker.

"What will you be up to today?" he asked, as he poured her a cup.

"I should probably work on unpacking. Although, considering my current employment situation, I might have to look into renting a cheaper place. Just until things are settled."

He handed her a steaming cup and she took a sip. The coffee was rich and full-bodied and tasted expensive.

He leaned back against the edge of the counter. "The offer for the job at the Royal Inn is still good. I can even work on getting you out of my office and into a management position sooner if that would sweeten the deal."

She wished she could, but that was no longer an option. The only reason she had even considered it in the first place was for her father's sake.

"You know I can't do that. But thank you. I do appreciate the offer." She leaned against the opposite counter. "What are you doing today?"

"Most likely damage control."

Well, that was awfully direct. Although she wasn't sure how she felt about him referring to their night together as *damage*.

Then he held up the front section of the newspaper and she realized he wasn't talking about them. The headline read in bold type:

*Royal Family Reveals Illegitimate Heir*

Beside the article was a photo of an attractive woman in her early to mid-thirties who bore a striking resemblance to the king. "Another illegitimate heir?"

"She's their half sister," Charles said. "The result of King Frederick's affair with the wife of the former prime minister."

As if his family hadn't had enough scandal the past couple of years. "Oh, boy."

"Yeah. It's not going to be pretty."

She took the page from him and skimmed the article. Not only was this princess illegitimate, but she was the oldest living heir. Which, the article stated, could mean that she was the rightful heir to the crown itself.

Did this mean King Phillip would lose the crown? A move like that could potentially turn the country upside down.

She was dying of curiosity. But as the family attorney, Charles probably wouldn't be able to tell her more than was divulged in the press release.

"This is what that meeting was about the other day, wasn't it?" she asked.

He nodded. "We wanted to get the press release out as soon as possible, before the tabloids caught wind of it."

From the other room she heard her cell phone ring. It was still in her purse on the couch. "I should get that," she said.

By the time she reached the living room, opened her purse, and wrestled her cell phone out, she'd missed the call. There was no name listed and the number was unfamiliar. Then the phone chirped to indicate that a message had been left. She would listen to it later.

There were also two calls from her father from the night before. Had he called to argue, or was he ready to apologize? She didn't even want to think about that right now.

She needed to get dressed and get back to her own place, before this got too cozy. Besides, she didn't want to wear out her welcome. It would be awkward if he had to ask her to leave.

"Everything okay?"

She turned to find Charles standing in the arch between the living room and the foyer, watching her. She snapped her phone shut and stuffed it back in her purse. "Probably just a wrong number."

"I was about to jump into the shower," he said, walking toward her. "I thought you might like to join me."

Oh, that was so tempting. He was obviously in no hurry to get rid of her. Would it hurt to stay just a little bit longer...?

"I really need to go," she told him.

He didn't push the issue, although if he had, she just might have caved.

"I have family obligations this evening," he said, "but I'm free Sunday night. How about dinner?"

She wondered if he really had family obligations or just some other woman he'd already made plans to see. Although, as far as she could tell, he'd never been anything but honest with her.

She just wasn't ready to trust him yet. "Call me."

He folded his arms across his chest. "Why do I get the feeling that means no?"

She shrugged. "It means call me."

But, in all honesty, it probably did mean no. Even so, she couldn't help wondering, as she headed upstairs to get dressed, if she didn't say yes, would it just be someone else?

The possibility that it might be disturbed her far more than it should have.

* * *

It was amazing that despite being only half Mead, Melissa Thornsby looked so much like her siblings. She had the same dark hair and eyes, and the same olive complexion. She was tall and slim, and she carried herself with that undeniable royal confidence. She even shared similar expressions and gestures. Charles couldn't help wondering: if she had stayed on Morgan Isle after her parents' death, would someone have made the connection years ago?

He stood off to the side of the palace library, where this first meeting was taking place, as introductions were being made. At times like this he couldn't help feeling like an outsider. And, yes, maybe a little envious. But he had his mother, who drowned him in so much attention he couldn't imagine when he would find time for anyone else. And people wondered why he insisted on staying single. He didn't think he could handle his mother *and* a wife demanding his time.

The only catch, he thought, as he watched Phillip cradle his son, was that someday he would like to have children of his own. Not that he needed to be married for that. But he'd seen firsthand what a mess an illegitimate child could cause in a royal family.

Melissa spotted him and walked over.

"You must be Charles." She spoke with an accent mottled with varying intonation. A touch of the New Orleans South combined with a twinge of East Coast dialect, and something else he couldn't quite put his finger on. Very unusual. Especially for a princess.

He nodded. "Welcome home, Your Highness."

She took his hand and clasped it warmly. She carried herself with a style and grace that reeked of old money and privilege. "I wanted to thank you for all you've done. For making all the arrangements."

He was just doing his job. But he smiled and said, "You're welcome."

"It's not every day one is informed they may have an entire family they know nothing about. It could have been messy. I was impressed by how diplomatically the situation was handled, and I'm told that was in most part due to you."

"I really can't take the credit."

"Modest," she said, with a smile. "A good quality." She glanced around the room, as though searching for something. "Is your spouse not here with you?"

"I'm not married."

"Significant other?"

Oddly enough, the first person who came to mind was Victoria. Odd because she was no more significant than any other woman he had dated. "No one special."

"A handsome thing like you," she teased in a deep Southern drawl. "Why, in New Orleans you'd have been snapped up by some lovely young debutante ages ago."

"I could say the same for you," he said. "How could a woman so lovely still be single?"

"Oh," she said, with a spark of humor lighting her eyes, "we won't even go there."

Despite the trepidation of the rest of the family, Charles knew without a doubt that he was going to like his cousin. She had spunk and a pretty damned good sense of humor. He appreciated a woman, especially one in her social position, who didn't take herself too seriously.

Sophie stepped up beside them. "Sorry to interrupt, but I thought I might show Melissa to her suite and get her settled in."

"I certainly could use a breather," Melissa said. "It's been something of a crazy week, to say the least." She turned to Charles. "It was a pleasure meeting you. I hope we see quite a bit more of each other."

"As do I," he said, and honestly meant it. He suspected that Melissa would make a very interesting, and entertaining, addition to their family.

When they were gone, he heard Ethan ask from behind him, "So, what do you think of her?"

Charles turned to him. "I like her."

"She's quite outspoken."

"I think that's the thing about her that I like. Maybe she'll stir things up a bit."

Ethan nodded thoughtfully, and Charles had the distinct impression he felt wary of his new sibling. Which surprised him, since Ethan himself was illegitimate. If anyone were to welcome her with open arms, he would expect Ethan to. Knowing of Melissa's vast wealth, surely they didn't suspect she might be after their fortune. She had also made assurances to her attorney that she had no interest whatsoever in taking her rightful place as ruler of the country. But before Charles could question his wariness, Ethan changed the subject.

"Have you made any progress convincing Victoria to stay?"

He shook his head. "I'm working on her, though. I

think I'll have her mind changed by my father's birthday party."

Ethan's brow perked with curiosity. "She'll be there?"

Charles knew exactly what Ethan was thinking. He would never come right out and ask if Charles had slept with her, but he obviously had his suspicions.

"My mother has taken a liking to her," Charles said. "When she suggested inviting her, I figured it would be the perfect opportunity for her to get to know the family. Maybe then she would be more willing to accept our offer."

It wasn't a complete lie, more a vast stretching of the truth, but Ethan seemed to buy it.

"Good thinking. I'll make sure the others know to expect her there."

So, in other words, they would tag-team her. Try to wear her down. It couldn't hurt.

"We should see that Melissa knows she's welcome, too," Ethan said.

"I'll have my mother ring her," Charles said. Or as Victoria said, his "smother." The endearment brought a smile to his face.

He'd dated a lot of women in his life, but Victoria was different. Maybe part of the fascination was that women usually chased him, and for the first time he found himself the pursuer. And the truth was he sort of liked it. He was enjoying the challenge for a change.

All his life, things had come very easily to him. He would be the first to admit that he'd been spoiled as a child. There had never been a single thing he'd asked for that he hadn't gotten. Even if his father had said no, his mother would go behind his back.

Being told no was a refreshing change. He saw Victoria as more of an equal than just another temporary distraction. Not that he expected it to last. But why not enjoy it while he could?

# Twelve

It was almost three in the afternoon when Victoria remembered the message on her cell phone and finally dialed her voice mail. As she listened to the somber voice on the other end, her heart plummeted and a cold chill sank deep into her skin, all the way through to her bones.

Her father had been admitted to the hospital with chest pains and was undergoing tests. The fact that the doctor had called, and not her father himself, filled her with dread. She called the hospital back but they refused to give her any information over the phone, other than to say that he was stable.

Was he unconscious? Dying? His cardiologist had warned that another attack, even a minor one, could do irreparable damage.

Hands trembling, heart thudding almost painfully hard in her chest, she threw on her jacket, grabbed her purse, and raced to Bay View Memorial Hospital as fast as the congested city streets would allow—damned tourists. She swore to herself that if he would just come out of this okay, she would never raise her voice to him, never be angry with him for as long as she lived.

And what if he wasn't okay? What if she got there and he was already gone? How would she ever forgive herself for those terrible things she'd said to him?

She'd lost her mum and her brother. She wasn't ready to lose him too. She couldn't bear it.

At the hospital information desk she was given a pass and directed to the cardiology wing on the fourth floor. When she reached the room, she was afraid to step inside, terrified of what she might see. Would it be like the last time? Her father hooked to tubes and machines?

With a trembling hand she rapped lightly on the door and heard her father's voice, strong and clear, call, "Come in."

She stepped inside, saw him sitting up in bed, his eyes bright and his color good, and went weak with relief. The machines and monitors she'd expected were nowhere to be seen. He didn't even have an IV line.

He was okay.

*For now, at least,* a little voice in her head said.

"Sweetheart," he said, looking relieved to see her. "I thought you were so angry with me you wouldn't come."

She thought she would be mad at him forever, but her anger just seemed to melt away. He held his arms out and she threw herself into them. She buried her face in the crook of his neck, squeezed him like she never wanted to let go, and he squeezed her right back.

"I'm sorry," they said at the exact same time.

"No," he said. "You had every right to be angry with me. I shouldn't have lied to you."

"It's okay."

"No, sweetheart, it isn't." He cupped her face in his hands. "I should have been honest with you from the start. I thought I was protecting you. And I was ashamed of the mess I'd made out of things."

"We all make mistakes."

He stroked her cheek with his thumb. "But I want you to know how deeply sorry I am. It's been just the two of us for a long time now. I would never do anything to intentionally hurt you."

"I know. It's all in the past now," she said. Hadn't losing the hotel been penalty enough? Was it fair to keep punishing him for his sins? And if she were the one who had made the mistake, wouldn't she want to be forgiven?

He was all she had left. They were a team. They had to stick together.

"What happened to you?" She sat on the edge of the bed and took one of his hands. It felt warm and strong. "Was it another attack?"

He shook his head, wearing a wry smile. "Acid reflux, the doctor said. Brought on by extreme stress. My cardiologist did a full workup just to be safe, and as far as they can tell I'm fit as a fiddle. They should be releasing me any time now."

She doubted *fit as a fiddle* was the term the doctor used. Probably more like *out of the woods*. "I'll wait around and take you home."

"Victoria, I also wanted to say I'm sorry that I was so rude to the duke. I guess I was just a little…surprised. He doesn't seem your type."

No kidding. It had been so long since she'd been in a relationship, she wasn't sure what her type was, anymore. And considering all her past disastrous relationships, maybe it was time to rethink exactly what her type should be.

"I wasn't sure about him at first," she told her father, "since he does have something of a reputation with women. But the truth is, he's not a bad guy. In fact, he's actually quite sweet. When he's not being arrogant and overbearing, that is."

"Is it…serious?"

She emphatically shook her head. "God, no. It's… *nothing*."

He gave her that fatherly *you can't fool me* look. "It didn't look like nothing to me. The way he came to the door to see if you were okay. He has feelings for you."

Not in the way her father suspected. "It isn't like that. We're keeping it casual. *Very* casual."

He raised a brow at her. "Let's face it, Vicki, you don't do casual very well. When you fall, you fall hard."

That used to be true, but she'd changed. The past few years, she hadn't fallen at all. She hadn't given herself the opportunity. She had pretty much sworn off men after her last catastrophic split.

It had been inevitable she would eventually take a

tumble off the celibacy wagon. She just never suspected that it would be with a man like Charles.

"This is different," she told him. "*I'm* different."

"I hope so. I know you think you're tough, but I've seen your heart broken too many times before."

She had no intention of putting herself back in that kind of situation. "Would you mind if we don't have a discussion about my love life? Besides, *your* heart is the one we should be worrying about."

He gave her hand a squeeze. "I'm going to make this up to you, Vicki. All the trouble I caused. I'm not sure how yet, but I will."

"I can take care of myself, Daddy." And if not, it was time she learned how. She'd been relying on him for too long.

All that mattered now was that he was alive and well, and they were back to being happy.

Victoria didn't see Charles again until Sunday night, when he showed up unannounced at her door. He looked delicious in dark slacks, a warm, brown cashmere sweater and a black leather jacket.

Any thoughts she had of turning him away evaporated the instant he smiled. She did love that smile.

"Inviting yourself over again?" she asked, just to give him a hard time.

"I tried calling today, but you didn't answer," he said, as if that were a perfectly logical reason.

"My phone died. I just plugged it in a few minutes ago when I got home."

"Are you going to let me in?"

Like she had a choice. She stepped aside and gestured him in. "Just for a few minutes."

He stepped inside, bringing with him the scent of the brisk autumn air. He took his jacket off and hung it over the back of the couch, then sat down. She sat beside him. Something about him being there was very…comfortable.

Or it could all be an illusion.

"You look tired," he said.

"It's been an exhausting weekend. My father was admitted to the hospital with chest pains Friday night."

He sat forward slightly, and the depth of concern on his face surprised her. "Is he all right?"

"He's fine. It wound up being his stomach, not his heart, but I stayed with him last night and all day today, just to be safe." And while it was nice spending time with him, it made her realize just how comfortable she'd become living alone. It had been something of a relief to get back to her flat. To her home and her things.

"I guess this means things are okay with you two."

She nodded. "It's amazing how a scare like that can alter your perception. When I imagined losing him forever, the rest of it all seemed petty and insignificant."

"You should have called me," he said.

"What for?"

He shrugged. "Support. Someone to talk to."

"Come on, Charles. You and I both know that isn't the way this works. We don't have that kind of relationship. We have sex."

He grinned. "Really great sex."

"Yes," she agreed. "And in the end, that's all it will ever be."

She could swear he looked almost…hurt. "Would it be such a stretch to think of me as a friend?"

If he were anyone else, no. "Until tomorrow, or the day after, when the next woman catches your eye and I get tossed aside? That isn't friendship."

He frowned. "That's a little unfair, don't you think?"

"Not at all. It's quite realistic, in fact. I mean, can you blame me? It's not as if you don't have a reputation for that sort of thing."

"What if I said, for now, I only want to see you."

At first she thought he was joking. Then she realized he was actually serious. "I guess I would say that you're delusional. You're totally incapable of a monogamous relationship."

"Hey, I've had relationships."

"Name the longest one."

He paused, his brow furrowing.

"That's what I thought."

"Maybe I want to try."

In a monogamous relationship, she gave him a week, tops. And that was being generous. "I don't want to get involved. I don't want a commitment." Especially with a man like him.

"Neither do I," he said. "We'll keep it casual."

"Casually exclusive? That doesn't even make sense."

"Sure it does. You've never dated someone just to date them, with no expectations."

Not really. Like her father said, when she fell, she fell hard. That was the way it was supposed to happen, as it did with her parents. They met, they fell in love, they settled down and started a family. But it had never quite seemed to work that way for her. Perhaps she'd been expecting too much?

Maybe this time it would be different. In the past she had entered relationships with the understanding, the expectation, that it would be long-lasting. And when it didn't work out she'd felt like a failure. But this was different. She was entering this relationship with no expectations at all.

"We're attracted to each other," Charles said. "And you can't deny that we're hot in bed."

She wouldn't even try.

"So," he asked. "Why not?"

He made it sound so simple. "How long?"

He shrugged. "Until it's not fun anymore, I suppose."

"Who says I'm having fun now?"

He flashed her that sexy grin. "Oh, I know you are."

Yeah, she was. The sex alone was worth her while.

But what if the only thing keeping Charles interested was the challenge, the thrill of the chase? If she gave in too easily, would he lose interest?

"I'll think about it," she said, and enjoyed the look of surprise on his face when she didn't bend to his will.

He opened his mouth to say something—God only knew what—but the bell for the door chimed.

Before she could move, he rose to his feet. "That's for me."

For him? Who would he invite to her flat?

"Back in a sec." He walked to the door. She heard him open it and thank whoever it was, then he reappeared with a large white box in his arms. The name of an exclusive downtown boutique was emblazoned on the top. Exclusively women's clothing.

What had he done this time?

"What is that?" she asked.

"A gift," he said, setting the box in her lap. It was surprisingly heavy. "I saw it in the shop window and knew I had to see you in it."

What had he done?

"Open it," he said eagerly, grinning like a kid at Christmas.

She pulled off the top and dug through layers of gold tissue paper until she encountered something royal blue and shimmering. She pulled it from the box and found herself holding a strapless, floor-length, sequined evening gown. It was so beautiful it took her breath away.

"Do you like it?" he asked.

"Charles, it's amazing, but—"

"I know, I know. You can afford your own dress and all that." He sat down beside her. "When I saw it in the shop window, I knew it would be perfect for you. And I can see already that it is."

He was right. If she'd had every gown in the world to choose from, she probably would have picked this very one. He'd even gotten the size right.

The price tag was missing, but she was sure that from this particular boutique, it must have cost a bundle. More than she could afford to spend.

"It's too much," she said.

"Not for me, it isn't."

Maybe this was one of the perks of dating a multimillionaire. Even though they weren't technically dating.

Normally she wouldn't accept a gift like this. But it was just so beautiful. So elegant. The designer was one she had always admired and dreamed of wearing, but never could quite fit into her budget.

She considered offering to pay him back, but God only knew when she would have the money. As it was, she was barely making the rent.

Maybe she could say yes, just this once.

"I love it," she said. "Thank you."

"The manager said if it needs altering, bring it around Monday and they'll put a rush on it. I wasn't sure about jewelry or shoes."

"That part I have covered," she said.

She could tell just from looking at it that at least three inches would have to go from the hem. She folded it carefully and lay it back in the box.

"Aren't you going to model it for me?" he asked.

She shook her head and eased the top back in place. "It will just have to be a surprise."

Something told her that if she wore it for him before the party, the novelty might wear off.

*See,* she told herself, *this is what you would have to look forward to if you let yourself get involved with him.* She would always be fretting about how to keep him interested, worrying that any minute he would get tired of her.

"Could I at least get a thank-you kiss?" he asked, tapping an index finger to his lips. "Right here."

"Just a quick one," she said. Then she would kick him out so she could get to bed early for a change. She had a lot of sleep to catch up on.

She leaned in and pressed her lips to his, but before

she could back away, he cupped a hand behind her head and held her there. And it felt so good, she only put up the tiniest bit of resistance before she gave in and melted into his arms.

One kiss turned into two kisses, which then led to some touching. Then their clothes were getting in the way, so naturally they had to take them off.

When he picked her up and carried her to the bedroom, she had resigned herself to another sleepless but sinfully satisfying night.

# Thirteen

Victoria sat with Charles in the back of the Bentley, her luggage for the weekend tucked beside his in the trunk. She had planned to drive herself to his parents's estate. But after a long week of Charles giving her every reason to make the hour-long drive with him—outrageous petrol prices, complicated directions, and who knew, maybe even highway robbery—she had finally relented and agreed to ride with him.

It wasn't as though she was concerned she wouldn't be welcomed. She and Charles's mother had practically become buddies over the past couple of weeks. Mrs. Mead had called every day as usual, but there were times when she called specifically to speak with Victoria, not Charles.

She wanted to know Victoria's preference for dinner

Friday night. Beef or fish? And which room would she prefer to stay in? One facing the ocean or the gardens? Did she prefer cotton sheets or silk, and were there any food allergies the cook should be aware of? Was there a special wine she would like ordered, or would she prefer cocktails? And the list went on. Victoria wondered if she was this attentive with all the guests who stayed with them.

With each call Mrs. Mead expressed how thrilled she and her husband were to be meeting Victoria. And even though Mrs. Mead never came right out and said it, Victoria couldn't escape the feeling that she was reading way more into Victoria and Charles's relationship than was really there. And Victoria was feeling as though she was being sucked into the family against her will. Which might not have been horrible if the man in question were anyone but Charles.

Yes, she and Charles had fun together—and not just the physical kind. He made her laugh, and she never failed to get that shimmy of excitement in her belly when he popped his head in her office or appeared unannounced at her door. But she still hadn't given him a definitive answer about the nature of their relationship.

And call her evil, but keeping him guessing gave her a perverse feeling of power. If she could just ignore the fact that she was coming dangerously close to falling for him. But she would never be that foolish. The instant she gave in, surrendered her will to him, the thrill of the chase would be gone, and Charles would lose interest.

Hopefully she would be long gone before then.

"By the way," she told him, "the employment agency

called just before we left. They have four more possible candidates for the assistant position."

"Splendid," he said. "Make interview appointments first thing next week."

"Why bother?" she asked wryly. "You haven't liked a single applicant yet."

They had all been perfectly capable. And not a gorgeous face or sexy figure in the lot of them. Which she suspected was the reason he'd dismissed them all without consideration.

"I'm sure the right one will come along," he said.

He or she would have to. Victoria's time was nearly up. At this rate she would have to stay longer to train whomever he hired, and she had other irons in the fire. In fact, she was expecting a very important phone call any day now that just might determine her immediate future plans. The opportunity of a lifetime, her father had said.

But she refused to let herself think about that and add even more nervous knots to the ones already twisting her stomach.

The hour-long drive seemed to fly by, and before she knew it they were pulling up to the gates of the estate. She noted it was not at all hard to find—one turn off the coastal highway and they were there.

And only then did she become truly nervous. What if they hated her? Made her feel like she was imposing? Would his parents smother Charles with affection and leave her feeling like the fourth wheel?

Things she maybe should have considered *before* she climbed into the damned car.

As they approached, the gates swung open. The car

followed the long, twisting drive, and she got her first view of his parents' estate. The home that she supposed would one day belong to Charles.

It was utterly breathtaking, and so enormous it made her father's estate look like a country cottage. Built sometime in the nineteenth century, the impressive structure sat on endless acres of rolling green lawns that tapered down to a stretch of private beach. The grounds were crawling with staff, all bustling with activity. To prepare for the party tomorrow night, she assumed.

"What do you think?" Charles asked.

"It's really something," she said, peering out her window. "Has it always been in the royal family?"

"Actually, this house comes from my mother's side. Her family originated on Thomas Isle, the sister island to Morgan Isle. They immigrated here in the late nine- teenth century."

"I didn't realize you had ties to Thomas Isle," she said. Up until recently, their respective monarchies had ruled in bitter discord with the other. As few as ten years ago they weren't even on speaking terms.

"Have you ever been there?" he asked, and she shook her head. "It's very different from Morgan Isle. Farming community, mostly, and a little archaic by our stan- dards. Although, in the last few years the entire island has gone with the recent green trend, and all the crops they export now are certified organic. We should go sometime, tour the island and the castle."

She wasn't sure how she felt about taking another trip with him, or the fact that he'd even suggested it. Here they were, going on four weeks of seeing each other, and he still wasn't making noise like he wanted out. The longer they dragged this out, the more attached they would become. Not to mention that if things worked out as she'd planned, she might not be on the island much longer.

The car slowed to a stop by the front entrance, and the driver got out to open the door for them.

As they stepped out into the brisk, salty ocean air, the front door opened and Charles's parents emerged. Victoria was struck instantly by what an attractive couple they made.

Mrs. Mead looked much younger than her husband, and that surprised Victoria. She'd imagined her older and more matronly. In reality Mrs. Mead looked youthful, chic, and stunningly beautiful. And though Mr. Mead was showing his age, he was brutally handsome and as physically fit as his wife. Nothing like the stodgy old man she's been picturing all this time. It was clear where Charles had gotten his good looks.

Talk about hitting the gene-pool jackpot! She could just imagine the gorgeous children she and Charles—

*Whoa.* Where had that errant and totally unrealistic thought come from? Talk about a cold-day-in-hell scenario. She didn't even know if Charles wanted children.

She didn't *want* to know. Because if the answer was yes, it would make him that much more appealing.

"Your parents are so handsome," she whispered to Charles. "I never imagined your mother would be so young."

"Don't let her face fool you," he whispered back. "She just has an exceptional plastic surgeon."

Victoria hung back a few steps as Mrs. Mead approached them, arms open, and folded her son into a crushing embrace. "It's so wonderful to see you, dear! Did you have a good trip?"

"Uneventful," he said, untangling himself from her arms so he could shake his father's hand. "Happy Birthday, Dad."

"Welcome home, son," his father said with a smile that lit his entire face. There was no doubt, they adored their child. Not that Victoria could blame them.

Charles gestured her closer. "Mum, Dad, this is my colleague, Victoria Houghton."

Victoria curtsied. "I'm so pleased to finally meet you both," she said, accepting Mr. Mead's outstretched hand, then his wife's.

"The pleasure is all ours, Victoria," his mother said, "And please, you must call us Grant and Pip."

Her name was *Pip?* Victoria bit her lip to hold back a nervous giggle.

"I know what you're thinking," Mrs. Mead, *Pip,* said. She looped an arm through Victoria's and led her toward the house. "What kind of a name is Pip?"

"It is unusual," she admitted.

"Well, my parent's weren't that eccentric. My given name is Persephone."

That wasn't exactly a name you heard every day, either.

"I don't know if Charles told you, but I used to be a runway model."

"No, he didn't." But that wasn't hard to believe. At least she hadn't put those looks and figure to waste.

"This was back in the sixties." She shot Victoria a wry smile. "I'm aging myself, I know. But anyway, those were the days of Twiggy. They liked them tall and ghostly thin. I was thin enough, but at five feet seven inches I wasn't exactly towering over the other models. So, because I was the shortest, everyone started calling me Pipsqueak. Then it was shortened to Pip. And that's what people have been calling me ever since. Isn't that right, Grant?"

"As long as I've known you," he agreed.

She didn't seem small, but then, with the exception of young children, everybody was taller than Victoria.

"My parents abhorred it, of course," Pip said, as they stepped through the door into the foyer, Charles and his father following silently behind. "But being something of a rebellious youngster, that only made the name more appealing."

The inside of their home was just as magnificent and breathtaking as the outside. Vaulted ceilings, antique furnishings, and oodles of rich, polished wood. So different from the modern furnishings in Charles's home. It was difficult to imagine him growing up here.

"I'll show you to your room so you can settle in," Pip said. "Then we can meet in the study for a drink before dinner. Grant, would you be a dear and check that Geoffery brought the correct wine up from the cellar?"

"Of course." He flashed Victoria a smile, then walked off in the opposite direction. If it bothered him being sent on errands, it didn't show.

"He's the wine connoisseur," Pip explained. "I'm more of a gin-and-tonic girl."

They climbed the stairs, Charles in tow, and Pip showed her to a room decorated in Victorian-era floral with what she assumed was authentic period furniture. A bit frilly for Victoria's taste, but beautiful.

A servant followed them in with Victoria's luggage.

"Would you like a maid to help you unpack?" Pip asked.

"No, thank you." She'd never been fond of total strangers rifling through her things—or even the maid who had been with her and her father for years.

"Well, then, is there anything you need? Anything I can get you?"

"I'm fine, thanks."

"Mum," Charles said, "why don't we leave Victoria to unpack? You can walk me to my room."

"If there's anything you need, anything at all, just buzz the staff." She gestured to the intercom panel by the door. "Twenty-four hours a day."

Jeez, talk about being smothered with kindness. "Thank you."

"Shall we meet in the study in an hour?"

"An hour is fine, Mum." Charles had to all but drag her from the room. And before he closed the door behind him, he told Victoria, "I'll be by to show you to the study, and later I'll take you on a tour."

The devilish look in his eyes said he had more than just a tour in mind.

"Charles, she's lovely!" his mother gushed the instant they were in his room. "So pretty and petite. Like a pixie."

"Don't let her size fool you. She can hold her own."

"Just the kind of woman you need," she said.

Could she be any *less* subtle?

He should have seen this coming. "Don't start, mother."

She shrugged innocently. She knew he meant business when he called her mother instead of Mum. "Start what, dear?"

"*Pushing* me."

She frowned. "Is it wrong to want to see my only son settle down? To hope for maybe a grandchild or two? I'm not getting any younger."

It was times like this he hated being an only child. "You're only fifty-eight."

She shot him a stern look. "Bite your tongue, young man."

So he added, "But you don't look a day over thirty-five."

She smiled and patted his cheek. "That's my sweet boy."

Ugh. He hated when she called him that. And she wondered why he didn't come around very often. He hoisted his suitcase up on the bed and unzipped it.

"Let a maid do that," she scolded.

"You know I prefer to do it myself."

She sighed dramatically, as though he was a lost cause, and sat on the bed to watch him. "You brought your tux?"

"Of course."

"And Victoria?"

"She would look terrible in a tux."

She gave him a playful shove. "You know what I mean."

"She's all set."

"I thought of offering her the use of one of my gowns, but she's at least two sizes smaller."

"I bought her a gown."

She raised a curious brow. "Oh, did you?"

"Don't go reading anything into it. I just wanted her to feel comfortable."

"It's been ages since you brought a date home."

"We're not dating," he said. Victoria's rules, not his. Although, if this wasn't dating, he wasn't sure what to call it. It was the longest exclusive relationship he'd ever had with a woman.

He'd kept waiting for it to lose its luster, to get bored with her. Instead, with every passing day, he seemed to care more for her. In a temporary way, that is.

"So what *are* you doing," she asked, and the instant the words were out, she held up a hand and shook her head. "On second thought, I don't want to know."

"She's a friend," he said, and realized it was true. A friend with benefits. The two roles had always been mutually exclusive in the past. He'd never even met a woman he would want to sleep with *and* call a friend. She was definitely unique.

And when the inevitable end came, he had the feeling he would miss Victoria.

After drinks in the study, Victoria, Charles, and his parents had a surprisingly pleasant dinner together. Victoria found Pip to be much less overbearing in person, and Grant was quiet but friendly. It was rare he got a word in edgewise, though.

Pip must have asked Victoria a hundred questions about her family and her career, despite the warning looks she kept getting from her husband and son.

"What?" she would ask them. "I'm just curious."

Victoria didn't mind too much, although around the time dessert was served, it was beginning to feel a little like the Spanish Inquisition. When the questions turned a little too personal, to the tune of "So, Victoria, do you think you'll want children someday?" Charles put the kabash on it by taking her on that tour he'd promised. Which ended—*surprise*—right back in her room between the covers. Which is where they stayed for the rest of the night.

They were up bright and early for breakfast at eight, then spent hours with his parents chatting and looking through family photos, taking a long walk through the gardens and along the shore. And Victoria couldn't have felt more welcome or accepted.

She had expected Pip to grow bored with her almost immediately and cast her aside in favor of spending time with her son. But Pip remained glued to Victoria's side right up until the moment everyone went upstairs to get dressed for the party.

Not that Victoria minded. She liked Pip. She was witty and bright. A lot like Charles, really. She could even imagine them becoming friends, but there wouldn't likely be a chance for that.

"My parents really like you," Charles said, as they walked up the stairs together.

"I like them, too. I never expected your mum to be so attentive, though. At least, not toward me. Shouldn't she be showering her son with affection?"

"When I'm not here, she's desperate to keep in touch. And when I'm here, we have a few hours to catch up, then we run out of things to say to each other. The novelty wears off, I guess."

That sounded like someone else she knew. Always wanting what he couldn't have. And once he got it, he grew easily bored.

He hadn't gotten bored with her yet. But he would. It was inevitable.

Or was it?

Given his pathetically short attention span when it came to women, if he was going to grow tired of her, wouldn't it have happened by now?

She shook the thought from her mind, and not for the first time. That was dangerous ground to wander into. A place where she would undeniably get her heart smashed to pieces.

God knew it had happened enough times before.

"The party starts in three hours," he said, when they reached the top of the stairs, where they would part ways and go to their own rooms. "How much time do you need to get ready?"

She didn't have to ask why he wanted to know. It was clear in his sinfully sexy smile. And she had to admit, making love in his parents' home in the middle of the afternoon did hold a certain naughty appeal.

She took his hand, weaving their fingers together. "Your place or mine?"

# Fourteen

Victoria sat on the edge of the bed, her stomach twisted into nervous knots as she waited for Charles to fetch her from her room. They were already half an hour late, no thanks to Charles, who had finessed his way into her bed, then wouldn't get back out. She'd had to practically dress him herself and shove him out the door.

Now that she was ready, with nothing to do but sit and think, she couldn't keep her mind off of those one hundred or so guests she was going to have to meet. And the fact that she barely knew a single one of them. And how out of place she could potentially feel. Even when she and her father still had a thriving business, this echelon of society had been far out of their reach.

She was so edgy that when Charles rapped on the door, she nearly jumped out of her skin.

*Here we go.*

She shot to her feet, adjusting her dress, making sure she looked her best. She took a deep cleansing breath, then blew it out and called, "Come in!"

The door opened and Charles appeared, looking unbelievably handsome in his tux. "We're late—we have to…" He trailed off the instant he laid eyes on her, and for one very long moment he just stood there and stared. She was wearing the dress he had picked and had complemented it with the diamond jewelry she had inherited from her mother. Simple, but elegant.

But why didn't he say something? She swallowed hard and picked nervously at the skirt of her dress. "Well?"

"You look…" He shook his head, as though searching for the right words. He opened his mouth to say something, then closed it again. Then he shrugged and admitted, "I'm speechless."

She bit her lip. "Speechless good or speechless bad?"

He stepped closer. "Victoria, there are no words for how amazing you look in that dress." He lifted a hand to touch her cheek, then he leaned forward and brushed his lips across hers. So sweet and tender. And something happened just then. Something between them shifted. She could see in his eyes that he felt it too. Their relationship had…*evolved,* somehow. Moved to the next level.

"Victoria," he said, and she knew deep down in her heart what he was about to say. He was going to tell her that he was falling in love with her. She could just *feel* it. Her heart skipped a beat or two, then picked up double time.

He came so close, then at the last minute, chickened out. "We should get downstairs now."

She nodded, and let him lead her downstairs. She couldn't blame him for being afraid to say the words, to admit his feelings. This was new ground for him. And maybe he was afraid of rejection. But if he had gone out on a limb and said the words, she would have told him that she was falling in love with him, too.

Victoria found herself thrust amidst the upper crust of Morgan Isle society. The beautiful people. The weird thing was, despite any preconceived notion she may have had, that was really all they were. Just people. Not a single one treated her as though she were below them. And if deep down any thought so, they were kind enough to keep it to themselves.

Pip made sure that Victoria was introduced to all the right people and whispered to her juicy bits of gossip about them that Victoria found disturbingly entertaining. One by one she was reintroduced to the members of the royal family, and each took the chance to not so subtly try to convince her to stay with the Royal Inn. All she would say was that she was considering her options. She had to admit it was tempting, especially now that it was obvious they'd hired her on merit and not because of her father. But at the same time, she felt she needed a fresh start. Maybe, though, if the other position fell through, or if Charles asked her not to leave…

Which she was beginning to think was more and more likely. It seemed as though he hadn't taken his eyes off of her for a single minute all evening. Every time she turned he was there, watching her with that hungry look in his eyes. And she knew exactly what he was thinking.

He liked her in the dress, but he couldn't wait to get her out of it.

And people were noticing. Especially the women who were volleying for his attention.

"He can't keep his eyes off you," Pip told her, wearing the hopeful and conspiratorial smile of a mother who was ready to marry off her son.

"I noticed" was all Victoria said.

"He keeps insisting that you two are just friends, but I've never seen him look at a woman that way."

Her words sent an excited shiver through Victoria. Maybe Charles really did love her.

He saw the two of them talking and walked up to them. "Victoria, would you dance with me?"

"Go ahead," Pip said, eagerly waving them away. Whatever had happened between Victoria and Charles upstairs, Pip seemed to be sensing it, too. And no doubt loving every second.

Charles offered his arm and led Victoria out on the dance floor. The band was playing a slow, sultry number. Charles pulled her close to him, gazing down into her eyes. She felt mesmerized.

"Having a good time?" he asked, and she nodded. "Don't tell my mother I said this, but you're the most beautiful woman here."

Whether it was true or not, he made her believe it was. He made her *feel* beautiful. He was the only man she'd ever been with who made her feel good about herself.

His eyes searched her face, settled on her lips. "You wouldn't believe how badly I want to kiss you right now."

She grinned up at him. "And you wouldn't believe how badly I'd like you to." But they had always had an unspoken agreement. No physical affection when they were out in public together. He was hiding the relationship from his family, and she was protecting herself from everyone else. She didn't want to be labeled another one of his flings. Only this didn't feel like a fling any longer. This was real.

"Maybe I should then," he said.

It seemed to happen in slow motion. He lowered his head, one excruciating inch at a time, while Victoria's heart leapt up into her throat. Then his lips brushed hers, right there on the dance floor in front of everyone, softly at first. Then he leaned in deeper, catching the back of her head in his hand.

It was like their first kiss all over again. Sexy and exciting, and oh so good. And people were looking. She could feel their curious stares.

Their secret affair was officially out, and she didn't even care. She just wanted this night to last forever. She wanted *them* to last forever.

They parted slowly, hesitantly, and she rested her cheek against his chest, realizing, as they swayed to the music, that she had never been so happy in all her life.

Maybe he was afraid to say the words, but she wasn't. For the first time in a long time, she wasn't afraid of anything.

"Charles," she whispered.

"Hmm?"

"I think I'm falling in love with you."

She waited for him to squeeze her tighter, to gaze down at her with love and acceptance.

Instead he went cold and stiff in her arms. It was like dancing with a store mannequin.

*You just surprised him,* she told herself. *Any second now he's going to realize how happy he was to hear those words.*

*Say something,* she begged silently. *Anything.* But he didn't. It would seem she'd managed to stun him speechless again.

This time in a bad way.

Her knees felt unsteady and dread filled her heart. It was more than clear by his reaction that he didn't feel the same way. And he wasn't too thrilled to know that she did.

She had done it again. Despite going into this affair with no expectations whatsoever, she still managed to fall for Charles and get her heart filleted in the process. How could she have been so foolish to believe he actually cared about her? That he'd changed? That she was any different from the many others who came before her?

A person would think she'd have learned by now.

Tears of humiliation burned her eyes, but she swallowed them back. She wouldn't give anyone there the satisfaction of learning she was just one of many whose hearts he'd crushed.

She looked up at him with what she was sure was a strained smile. Her face felt like cold, hard plastic. "Thanks for the dance. Now, if you'll excuse me."

She broke away from him and walked blindly from the room, wanting only to get the hell out of there. She didn't even care that people were interrupting their conversations to stop and watch her pass. And she did her best to smile cordially, and nod in greeting.

So no one would realize she was dying inside.


"What did you do?" his mother hissed from behind him, as Charles helplessly watched Victoria walk away.

He turned to her, and under his breath said, "Stay out of this, Mother."

"Whatever you said to her, the poor girl went white as a sheet."

"I didn't say a thing." And that was the problem.

He shook his head and cursed under his breath. This was not his fault. Why did she have to go and say something like that? They had such a good thing. Why ruin it? And how in the hell had she gone from refusing to accept even a temporary exclusivity to falling in love with him? It made no sense.

Maybe she had just gotten caught up in the moment. That was probably it, he realized, feeling relieved. He needed to talk to her, before this thing was blown way out of proportion.

He started to walk away and his mother grabbed hold of his sleeve. "Sweetheart, everything inside me says she's the woman for you. And deep down I think you know it, too. *Why* won't you let yourself feel it?"

He pulled his arm free. "Excuse me, Mother."

He took the stairs two at a time. Her bedroom door was closed, so he knocked and called, "Victoria, I need to speak with you."

He didn't really expect a response, but he heard her call back, "Come in."

She was standing beside the bed, her suitcases open in front of her. She had changed out of her dress and it was draped across the footboard.

"What are you doing?" he asked.

"I thought I would get a head start on my packing," she said, but she wouldn't look him in the eye. She gestured to the dress. "You may as well take that. I'll never have a need for it again. Maybe someone else can get some use out of it."

He knew in that instant that she meant what she said, she was falling in love with him.

"Victoria, I'm sorry."

She bit her lip and shook her head. "No, it's my fault. I never should have said that to you. I don't know what I was thinking. Temporary insanity."

"You didn't give me a chance to say anything."

"Your silence said it all, believe me."

"I'm sorry. I'm just not—"

"In love with me? Yeah, I got that."

"We agreed this was temporary."

"You're absolutely right."

"It's not that I don't care for you."

She finally turned to him. "Look, this was bound to

happen, right? It's a miracle we lasted this long. It was going to end eventually."

"It doesn't have to," he said. They could just go back to the way things have been.

"Yes," she told him, "it does."

They were doing the right thing, so why did it feel like a mistake? "I feel…really bad."

She nodded sympathetically, but her eyes said she felt anything but. "That must be awful for you."

"You know that isn't what I mean."

"Look, I appreciate you coming after me and all. But honestly, you didn't do anything wrong. You did what you always do. And I should have expected that."

Maybe this wasn't her fault. Maybe he…led her on somehow. Made her believe he felt more that was really there.

She walked past him to the door and held it open. "Please leave."

"You're kicking me out?"

She nodded. "I created this mess. Now it's time I fixed it."

The drive back to the city the next morning was excruciatingly silent. Charles tried to talk to Victoria, to reason with her, but she refused to acknowledge him. The worst part wasn't even that she wasn't acting angry or wounded. She was just…cold.

He didn't follow her up to her flat when the car dropped her off, convinced that if he gave her time to cool off, she would see reason. But by eleven a.m. Monday he hadn't heard a word from her and she hadn't shown up at work. He checked her office to see if she'd slipped quietly in without him hearing her, and he realized all of her things were gone.

*What the hell?*

She was pissed at him. He got that. But that didn't mean she could just quit her job, just…*abandon* him.

He grabbed his jacket from his office and stormed out past Penelope, tossing over his shoulder, "Cancel all of my appointments."

Her car was parked out in front of her building, and he took the stairs two at a time up to her floor. He rapped hard on her door and barked, "Victoria!"

She opened the door, but left the security chain on. "What do you want?"

She looked tired, and the anger that had driven him there fizzled away.

"You didn't come to work," he said. "I was concerned."

"Technically, my three weeks are up. I don't work there anymore."

"But we haven't found a replacement yet. Who will do the training?"

"I'm sure you'll manage."

But that hadn't been the deal. And he didn't like being exiled in the hall. The least she could do was invite him in. She owed him that much. "Are you going to let me in?"

She hesitated, then she unlatched the chain and stepped aside to let him pass. "Only for a minute. I have a lot of packing to do."

"Packing? Are you going on a trip?"

"I'm moving."

She had said something about having to get a cheaper place. If she would just accept the damned job at the Royal Inn, she could stay right here. Or hell, she could probably afford to buy a house. "Where are you moving to?"

"London."

"England?"

"I was offered a position at a five-star hotel there. I start next Monday."

"You're leaving the country?"

"This Friday." She paused and said, "You could congratulate me."

*Congratulate* her? Wait. This was all wrong. She wasn't supposed to find a new job. She was supposed to change her mind and agree to work at the Royal Inn. "Whatever they're paying you, the Royal Inn will top it."

"I told you weeks ago, I don't want to work at the Royal Inn."

"But they want you. They're counting on me to convince you to stay."

"You'll just have to tell them you failed."

"It doesn't work that way. You can't leave."

She seemed to find his predicament amusing. "Look, I know you're used to getting your way, getting everything your heart desires, but this time you're just going to have to suck it up like the rest of us."

"It's not about that."

"Then what *is* it about, Charles? Because to me it sounds like you're just being a sore loser."

What was he trying to say? What did he really want from her?

He stepped toward her as though he could bully her to comply.

She didn't even flinch.

"You can't leave."

"Why? What can you offer me if I stay? A real relationship?"

"What we have is real."

"A commitment?"

He cringed. "Why do we have to do that? Why do we have to put a label on it? Why can't we just keep doing what we're doing?"

"Because that isn't what I want."

"It was a week ago. And why not? It was the perfect relationship. Totally uncomplicated."

Her expression darkened. "For you, maybe it was. But I'm tired of always being on edge. Waiting around for the other shoe to fall, for you to get bored and dump me. I just can't do it anymore."

"So you're dumping me first, is that it?"

She shrugged. "Welcome to the world of the dumpee. It's not fun, but trust me when I say you'll get over it."

She was right. He was usually the one to do the leaving. The one to walk away. So this was how it felt.

He knew that if he let her go, he would probably never see her again. But what choice did he have? She was right. It was very likely that in time he would grow tired of their relationship and need something else. He would feel trapped and stifled and get that burning need to move on. Then he would hurt her all over again.

It would be cruel and selfish to try to persuade her to stay. So he didn't.

He turned and left, walked away from her for the last time, an odd ache, like a spear thrust through his chest, making it hard to breath.

*It's just that your pride has been slightly bruised,* he assured himself. In a day or two he'd be fine. And when Victoria left, he wouldn't say a single damned thing to stop her.

# Fifteen

When Charles's doorbell chimed late Thursday afternoon, he was sure it was Victoria, there to tell him that she'd changed her mind. But instead he found Ethan standing on his front porch.

Ethan looked Charles up and down, took in his disheveled hair, wrinkled clothes, and four days' growth of facial hair. "Christ almighty, you look like hell."

Appropriately so, considering that was how he felt.

He stepped aside so Ethan could come in, then shut the door behind him. "I think I caught some kind of bug."

"I hope it's nothing catching," Ethan said warily. "Lizzy will kill me if I bring germs home. She's due any minute now, you know."

Only if wounded pride had become contagious. "I think you're safe."

"Could this have something to do with Victoria? Word is she took a job in England." At Charles's surprised look, Ethan said, "Did you think we wouldn't hear? I guess you didn't manage to convince her to stay, huh? And the way you were locking lips at the party, I'm guessing you ignored our request that you not sleep with her."

"Are you angry?"

He shrugged. "Let's just say I'm not surprised."

"If it counts for anything, I don't think it would have made a difference. Victoria Houghton is the most stubborn woman alive."

He walked to the kitchen, where he'd left his drink, and Ethan followed him. "What are you doing here, anyway?"

"You missed our squash game, genius. I called your office and your secretary said you've been out since last Friday."

"Yeah." Charles sipped his scotch and gestured to the bottle. "Want one?"

Ethan shook his head. "So, what happened?"

"I told you, I caught a bug."

"She dumped you, didn't she?"

Charles opened his mouth to deny it, but he just didn't have the energy.

Ethan flashed him a cocky grin and gave him a slap across the back. "The notorious Charles Mead was finally set loose by a woman. I never thought I would see the day. And she's moving all the hell the way over to England to get the away from you."

Charles glared at him. "I'm glad I could be a source of amusement."

"Welcome to the real world, my friend."

"Go to hell."

Ethan laughed. "What I find even more amusing, is that you're in love with her, and you probably didn't have the guts to tell her."

"I don't do love."

"Everyone does eventually."

"I'm not looking for a commitment," he insisted, but the familiar mantra was beginning to lose its luster. And the idea of being with anyone but Victoria left a hollow feeling in his gut.

That would pass.

"I know you see marriage as some kind of prison sentence, and I find that tragic. My life didn't truly begin until I married Lizzy."

Charles wanted to believe that it might be that way for him, too. It just seemed so far out of the realm of reality.

"You want to reschedule our game?" Ethan asked. "Or do you plan to mope in here for the rest of your life?"

"I'm not moping." Maybe he was a little depressed. Maybe it had been a slight shock to his system. But in a few days he would be back on his game. Besides, Victoria could still change her mind. She could realize that he was right and accept their relationship on his terms.

*You just keep telling yourself that, pal.*

Ethan's cell phone rang. He unclipped it from his belt and checked the display. "It's Lizzy." He flipped it open and said, "Hey, babe." He was silent for several seconds, then his eyes lit. "Are you sure?" Another pause, then, "Okay, I'll be there as soon as I can. Ten minutes, tops. Just hold on." He snapped his phone shut, grinning like an idiot. "Lizzy is in labor. Her water just broke." He laughed and slapped Charles on the back. "I'm going to be a father."

"Congratulations," Charles said, practically knocked backward by the intensity of Ethan's joy. What would it feel like to be that happy?

But he already knew the answer to that. He'd been that happy for a while. With Victoria. Right up until the instant when he'd screwed it all up.

Maybe he did love her. Maybe this so-called bug he'd contracted was really just lovesickness. Maybe his mum was right, and Victoria was the woman for him. Was it possible?

"You okay?" Ethan asked, wearing a concerned look. "You just got the weirdest expression on your face."

"Yeah," Charles said, unable to stifle the smile itching at the corners of his mouth. The same kind of goofy, lovesick smile Ethan had been wearing seconds ago. And he liked it. It felt…good. "I'm okay. In fact, I think I'm pretty great right now."

"If I didn't know any better, I would say you just came to your senses."

Maybe he did. Instead of feeling trapped or stifled, he felt free.

"What are you still doing here," he said, giving Ethan a shove in the direction of the foyer. "Are you forgetting your wife is waiting for you? You're going to be a father!"

Ethan grinned and looked at his watch. "How fast do you think I can get from here to the palace?"

"It's a twenty-minute drive, so probably about five. Now get out of here."

"I'm already gone," Ethan said, and Charles thought, with a chuckle, *Me too*.

As she was emptying the drawer of her bedside table into a box, Victoria saw the corner of a sheet of paper wedged between the headboard and mattress.

Probably just a magazine insert or an old message slip. She almost left it there, figuring it would fall loose when the movers took her bed apart. Then something compelled her to wedge her hand into the tight space and catch the corner of the paper with the tips of her fingers. When she pulled it free, and saw what it was, she wished she had just left it the hell alone.

It was an old shopping list, but what stopped her heart for an instant is what she found scribbled on the opposite side; the note that Charles had left her that first night they spent together.

It must have slipped off the pillow and gotten caught. Reading it now, in Charles chicken-scratch scrawl, sent a sharp pain through her heart.

Victoria,
Have an early meeting but wanted to let you sleep. I had a great time last night. See you in the office.
XOXO
Charles
P.S. Dinner tonight?

She'd managed, up until just then, not to shed a single tear over him. But now she felt the beginnings of a precariously dammed flood welling up against the backs of her eyes.

Some silly part of her that still believed in fairy-tale endings actually thought he might come after her. That he might have a sudden epiphany, like a lightning bolt from the heavens, and realize that he was madly in love with her. That he couldn't live without her.

Well, that certainly hadn't happened. She hadn't seen or heard from him since Sunday when he walked out of her apartment without even saying goodbye.

"Victoria?"

She turned to see her dad standing in the bedroom doorway. "Yeah?"

His brow was wrinkled with concern. He'd been worried about her lately, claimed that she wasn't acting like herself. He even hinted that by taking this job she might be running away from her problems, rather than facing them. Sort of like he had done.

She was seriously wondering the same thing. But it was too late to back out now.

"Everything okay?" he asked.

She nodded, a little too enthusiastically, and stuffed the note in the pocket of her jeans. "Fine, Daddy."

"The movers called. They'll be here tomorrow at eight a.m."

"Great." But it wasn't great. She didn't want to move to England and leave the only home she'd ever known. But careerwise, there wasn't much left for her here. The Royal Inn was the biggest game on the island, and she definitely had no future there.

"Almost finished in here?" he asked, the worry still

set deeply in his face. She wished there was something she could do to ease his mind. This shouldn't have to be so hard on him. But she knew he felt responsible for sticking her in this position in the first place.

"I think I'll need one more box for the closet stuff," she said. "Other than that, it's pretty much packed."

The bell rang and her father gestured behind him. "You want me to get that?"

"Would you mind? And could you grab me a box while you're out there?"

"Sure thing, honey."

Her father had wanted to move to England with her right away, but she asked him to wait until she was settled and had her bearings. And she wanted time to find them a nice place. Preferably something close to the hotel. With her new salary, signing bonus and moving expense account, as long as she stayed out of Central London, money wasn't going to a problem. It was her chance to finally take care of him. And he deserved it.

She dumped the rest of the drawer contents into the box, then carried it over to the closet. She still had room for a few pairs of shoes.

She heard a noise in the bedroom doorway, and turned to her father, asking, "Did you get me a b—" Then she realized that it wasn't her father standing there.

It was Charles.

Her knees went instantly soft, and her heart surged up and lodged somewhere near her vocal chords.

He looked so good, so casually sexy it made her chest sting. And what was he doing here?

"I don't have a *buh*. But I do have a *box*," he said, holding it out to her. "Your father asked me to bring it in."

Her father actually let him into the apartment? Couldn't he have asked first? What if she didn't want to talk to him?

*But you do,* a little voice in her head taunted. *You're dying to know why he's here.*

He probably just came to say goodbye. To wish her the best of luck in her new life.

When she didn't step forward and take the box from him, he dropped it on the floor. "Your dad told me to tell you that he was heading home for the night, and he would be back tomorrow around seven."

Great, he left her to deal with this alone. Way to be supportive, Dad.

"I'm a little busy right now," she said.

He nodded, hands wedged in the pockets of his slacks, gazing casually around the naked room. "I can see that. It looks as though you're all ready to go."

"The movers will be here tomorrow morning at eight." Why had she told him that? So he could show up at the last minute and beg her not to go? Like *that* would ever happen.

"So, you're really going?" he said.

Did he think this was all for show? An elaborate hoax to throw him off her scent? "Yes, I'm *really* going."

The jerk had the gall to look relieved! Like her leaving was the best thing that had ever happened to him.

"I'm glad my eminent departure is such a source of happiness for you," she snapped, when on the inside her heart was breaking all over again. Why couldn't he just leave her alone?

"I am happy," he admitted. "But not for the reason you think."

Getting rid of her wasn't reason enough? "Let me guess, you have a new girlfriend. Or six?" *Way to go, Ace, make him think you're jealous.* She needed to keep her mouth shut.

"I'm happy," he said, walking toward her, "because for some reason I can't even begin to understand, knowing that you're really leaving makes me realize how damned much I love you, Victoria."

He said it so earnestly, that for a second she almost believed him. But this had nothing to do with love. Real or imagined. "You only want me because you can't have me. Give it time. You'll find someone to fill the void, then you'll forget all about me."

"Forget you?" he said with a wry laugh. "I can't even fathom the idea of being with another woman."

"For now, maybe."

He shook his head. "No, this is not a temporary state of mind. This is it. You're stuck with me, until death do us part."

*Death do us part?* Was he talking *marriage?* Charles? Who spent his life bucking the very thought of the institution?

She narrowed her eyes at him, unable to let herself believe it. Yet there was a tiny kernel of hope forming inside of her, that made her think, *Maybe, just maybe…*

She folded her arms across her chest, eyed him suspiciously. "Who are you, and what have you done with Charles?"

"This is your fault," he said. "If you weren't everything I could possibly want in a woman, we wouldn't even be having this conversation. I would still be living happily oblivious and totally unaware of how freaking fantastic it feels to realize you've met the person you want to spend the rest of your life with."

"I don't believe you," she said, although with a pathetic lack of conviction.

He just smiled. "Yes you do. Because you know I would never lie to you. And I would never say something like this if I didn't mean it."

She swallowed hard, those damned tears welling in her eyes again. But at least this time they were happy. "Does this mean I don't have to go to England?"

"I was really hoping you wouldn't."

"Thank God!" she said, throwing herself into his open arms. And she had that same feeling, the one she'd had the first time she kissed him.

He was the one.

She was exactly where she was supposed to be.

His whole body seemed to sigh with relief, and he rested his chin on the top of her head. "I love you, Victoria."

She squeezed him, thinking, you are not going to cry, you big dope. But a tear rolled down her cheek anyway. "I love you, too."

"I'm sorry it took me so long to come to my senses."

"You know what they say. The things we have to work hardest for, we end up appreciating more." It sure made her appreciate him.

"Since you're not going to London, how would you feel about that position at the Royal Inn."

She looked up at him and grinned. "When do I start?"

"I'll talk to Ethan tomorrow." He lowered his head, rubbed his nose against hers. "You realize this means you'll have to deal with my mother a lot more now. She's going to go into anaphylactic shock when she hears I'm finally settling down. Which reminds me…" He rifled around in his pocket. "You want to give me a little room, so I can do this right?"

She backed away from him, wondering what he was up to now, then she saw the small velvet box resting in his palm. Then he actually lowered himself down on *one knee*.

*Oh, my God.*

He flipped the box open and in a bed of royal blue velvet sat a diamond ring that made her gasp. Not only was the stone enormous, but it sparkled like a star in the northern sky.

"It's beautiful."

"It was my grandmother's," he said. "Given to me when she died, to give to the woman I chose to be my wife. And until I met you, I didn't think there was a finger in the world I would ever want to place it."

That was, by far, the sweetest thing anyone had ever said to her. And she was pathetically close to a complete emotional meltdown. Her head was spinning and her hands were trembling and she had a lump in her throat the size of small continent.

"Victoria, will you marry me?"

She knew if she dared utter a sound she would dissolve into tears, so she did the next best thing.

She dropped to her knees, threw her arms around Charles and hugged him.

He laughed and held her tight. "I'll take that as a yes."

\* \* \* \* \*

*Don't miss ROYAL SEDUCER,*
*Part of the* MAN OF THE MONTH *continuity*
*available from Desire in July 2009.*

*Celebrate 60 years of pure reading pleasure with
Harlequin® Books!*

*Harlequin Romance® is celebrating by showering
you with DIAMOND BRIDES in February 2009.
Six stories that promise to bring a touch of sparkle to
your life, with diamond proposals and dazzling
weddings, sparkling brides and gorgeous grooms!*

*Enjoy a sneak peek at Caroline Anderson's
TWO LITTLE MIRACLES,
available February 2009 from Harlequin Romance®.*

'I've found her.'

Max froze.

It was what he'd been waiting for since June, but now—now he was almost afraid to voice the question. His heart stalling, he leaned slowly back in his chair and scoured the investigator's face for clues. 'Where?' he asked, and his voice sounded rough and unused, like a rusty hinge.

'In Suffolk. She's living in a cottage.'

*Living.* His heart crashed back to life, and he sucked in a long, slow breath. All these months he'd feared—

'Is she well?'

'Yes, she's well.'

He had to force himself to ask the next question. 'Alone?'

The man paused. 'No. The cottage belongs to a man

called John Blake. He's working away at the moment, but he comes and goes.'

God. He felt sick. So sick he hardly registered the next few words, but then gradually they sank in. 'She's got *what?*'

'Babies. Twin girls. They're eight months old.'

'Eight—?' he echoed under his breath. 'They must be his.'

He was thinking out loud, but the P.I. heard and corrected him.

'Apparently not. I gather they're hers. She's been there since mid-January last year, and they were born during the summer—June, the woman in the post office thought. She was more than helpful. I think there's been a certain amount of speculation about their relationship.'

He'd just bet there had. God, he was going to kill her. Or Blake. Maybe both of them.

'Of course, looking at the dates, she was presumably pregnant when she left you, so they could be yours, or she could have been having an affair with this Blake character before…'

He glared at the unfortunate P.I. 'Just stick to your job. I can do the math,' he snapped, swallowing the unpalatable possibility that she'd been unfaithful to him before she'd left. 'Where is she? I want the address.'

'It's all in here,' the man said, sliding a large envelope across the desk to him. 'With my invoice.'

'I'll get it seen to. Thank you.'

'If there's anything else you need, Mr. Gallagher, any further information—'

'I'll be in touch.'

'The woman in the post office told me Blake was away at the moment, if that helps,' he added quietly, and opened the door.

Max stared down at the envelope, hardly daring to open it, but when the door clicked softly shut behind the P.I., he eased up the flap, tipped it and felt his breath jam in his throat as the photos spilled out over the desk.

Oh, lord, she looked gorgeous. Different, though. It took him a moment to recognise her, because she'd grown her hair, and it was tied back in a ponytail, making her look younger and somehow freer. The blond highlights were gone, and it was back to its natural soft golden-brown, with a little curl in the end of the ponytail that he wanted to thread his finger through and tug, just gently, to draw her back to him.

Crazy. She'd put on a little weight, but it suited her. She looked well and happy and beautiful, but oddly, considering how desperate he'd been for news of her for the past year—one year, three weeks and two days, to be exact—it wasn't only Julia who held his attention after the initial shock. It was the babies sitting side by side in a supermarket trolley. Two identical and absolutely beautiful little girls.

\* \* \* \* \*

When Max Gallagher hires a P.I. to find his estranged wife, Julia, he discovers she's not alone—

she has twin baby girls, and they might be his. Now workaholic Max has just two weeks to prove that he can be a wonderful husband and father to the family he wants to treasure.

*Look for TWO LITTLE MIRACLES by*
*Caroline Anderson,*
*available February 2009 from Harlequin Romance®.*

# CELEBRATE
# 60 YEARS
OF PURE READING PLEASURE
WITH **HARLEQUIN**®!

We'll be spotlighting a different series
every month throughout 2009
to celebrate our 60th anniversary.

**Look for Harlequin® Romance in February!**

**Harlequin® Romance is celebrating by showering
you with Diamond Brides in February 2009.**

Six stories that promise to bring a touch of sparkle to
your life, with diamond proposals and dazzling weddings,
sparkling brides and gorgeous grooms!

Collect all six books in February 2009,
featuring *Two Little Miracles* by Caroline Anderson.

*Look for the Diamond Brides miniseries
in February 2009!*

**www.eHarlequin.com**     HRBRIDES09

# HARLEQUIN® Romance®

This February the Harlequin® Romance series
will feature six Diamond Brides stories featuring
diamond proposals and gorgeous grooms.

## *Share your dream wedding proposal and you could WIN!*

The most romantic entry will win a diamond
necklace and will inspire a proposal in one of
our upcoming Diamond Grooms books in 2010.

In 100 words or less, tell us the most romantic
way that you dream of being proposed to.

For more information, and to enter
the Diamond Brides Proposal contest, please visit
**www.DiamondBridesProposal.com**

Or mail your entry to us at:

IN THE U.S.: 3010 Walden Ave., P.O. Box 9069, Buffalo, NY 14269-9069
IN CANADA: 225 Duncan Mill Road, Don Mills, ON M3B 3K9

# REQUEST YOUR FREE BOOKS!

## 2 FREE NOVELS PLUS 2 FREE GIFTS!

**Silhouette Desire**

### Passionate, Powerful, Provocative!

**YES!** Please send me 2 FREE Silhouette Desire® novels and my 2 FREE gifts (gifts are worth about $10). After receiving them, if I don't wish to receive any more books, I can return the shipping statement marked "cancel". If I don't cancel, I will receive 6 brand-new novels every month and be billed just $4.05 per book in the U.S. or $4.74 per book in Canada, plus 25¢ shipping and handling per book and applicable taxes, if any*. That's a savings of almost 15% off the cover price! I understand that accepting the 2 free books and gifts places me under no obligation to buy anything. I can always return a shipment and cancel at any time. Even if I never buy another book, the two free books and gifts are mine to keep forever.

225 SDN ERVX  326 SDN ERVM

| | | |
|---|---|---|
| Name | (PLEASE PRINT) | |
| Address | | Apt. # |
| City | State/Prov. | Zip/Postal Code |

Signature (if under 18, a parent or guardian must sign)

### Mail to the Silhouette Reader Service:
**IN U.S.A.:** P.O. Box 1867, Buffalo, NY 14240-1867
**IN CANADA:** P.O. Box 609, Fort Erie, Ontario L2A 5X3

Not valid to current subscribers of Silhouette Desire books.

**Want to try two free books from another line?**
**Call 1-800-873-8635 or visit www.morefreebooks.com.**

\* Terms and prices subject to change without notice. N.Y. residents add applicable sales tax. Canadian residents will be charged applicable provincial taxes and GST. Offer not valid in Quebec. This offer is limited to one order per household. All orders subject to approval. Credit or debit balances in a customer's account(s) may be offset by any other outstanding balance owed by or to the customer. Please allow 4 to 6 weeks for delivery. Offer available while quantities last.

**Your Privacy:** Silhouette Books is committed to protecting your privacy. Our Privacy Policy is available online at www.eHarlequin.com or upon request from the Reader Service. From time to time we make our lists of customers available to reputable third parties who may have a product or service of interest to you. If you would prefer we not share your name and address, please check here. ☐

SDES08R

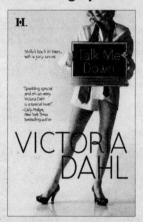

# COMING NEXT MONTH

### #1921 MR. STRICTLY BUSINESS—Day Leclaire
*Man of the Month*
He'd always taken what he wanted, when he wanted it—but she wouldn't bend to those rules. Now she needs his help. His price? Her—back in his bed.

### #1922 TEMPTED INTO THE TYCOON'S TRAP—
Emily McKay
*The Hudsons of Beverly Hills*
When he finds out that her secret baby is really his, he demands that she marry him. But their passion hasn't fizzled, and soon their marriage of convenience becomes very real.

### #1923 CONVENIENT MARRIAGE, INCONVENIENT
HUSBAND—Yvonne Lindsay
*Rogue Diamonds*
She'd left him at the altar eight years ago, but now she needs him in order to gain her inheritance. Could this be his chance to teach her that one can't measure love with money?

### #1924 RESERVED FOR THE TYCOON—Charlene Sands
*Suite Secrets*
His new events planner is trying to sabotage his hotel, but his attraction to her is like nothing he's ever felt. Will he choose to destroy her...or seduce her?

### #1925 MILLIONAIRE'S SECRET SEDUCTION—
Jennifer Lewis
*The Hardcastle Progeny*
On discovering a beautiful woman's intentions to sue his father's company, he makes her a deal—her body in exchange for his silence.

### #1926 THE C.O.O. MUST MARRY—Maxine Sullivan
Their fathers forced them to marry each other to save their families' fortunes. Will a former young love blossom again, or will secrets drive them apart?